The Bolo Dance

The Honey Strait Series Book 1

Paige Lynn Hill

TRS BOOKS

Patricia Hoving

The Bolo Dance

First published by TRS Books 2019

Copyright © 2019 by Paige Lynn Hill

This novel is entirely a work of fiction. The names, characters, and incidents portrayed in it are the work of the author's imagination. Any resemblance to actual persons, living or dead, events or localities is entirely coincidental.

All the lyrics and song titles contained within belong to their prospective songwriters.

First edition

Cover art by Getcovers Designs

This book was professionally typeset on Atticus.io

This book is dedicated to all of my women readers fighting to get back to what they love, even when life gets in the way.

AISO BY TRS BOOKS

PARANORMAL ROMANCE

A Bite Lurkers Novel series is a heartfelt vampiric romance about love, loss, and a hard look at that poignant phrase, *I'll love you forever.*

Dark Flames

Dark Modern

Dark Trade

DARK ROMANCE

The University Alley series is a dark erotic romance about a teacher who falls in love with her student who is battling a Heroin addiction.

Another Vice

Another Virtue

STANDALONES

A Songwriter's Death

A contemporary rockstar romance, where Tina and Michael both have been bitten by the fame bug. But when one reaches the promise land first it calls into questions their whole relationship and their life.

AND MORE BOOKS TO COME!

Contents

Prologue

Seven. That's how old I was when I first experienced rage. I used to wonder if that age range was normal. Then I had a toddler and I kind of knew anything was possible. Babies have an excuse because they don't know how to control their emotions. But that wasn't my problem.

Like a fire-breathing dragon, I was out for blood. The whole room was enveloped in a thin filter of red the day my dad had found the doll that I had been hiding. His very touch was already muddying up her pink Easter dress. Eliciting a scream from me that could shatter bulletproof glass.

"Damn it, Shannon! I told you not to buy the girl any dolls." He threw the doll in the trash. Turning back towards my Aunt and me as he undid his belt. No doubt to give me a whooping for my screaming. "Now look at her. She's all unruly."

"James, be reasonable," Shannon pleaded, getting up to block his path to me.

I ran straight to my room and the only toy I was allowed to have. A pair of bright, red boxing gloves. Shoving them onto my hands as best I could.

My dad who had taken my place on the couch stood up. "What's this now?"

"Patty was my dolly," I said through my tears while pummeling him in the legs. He only found it amusing. Still, I managed to get off a lucky shot to his private parts. Sending him to his knees.

My auntie just laughed from somewhere behind me. But I was far from being worried about getting in trouble. Landing another punch across his jaw. I now know, he fell back out of effect. However, he underestimated the space between the couch and the table. Hitting his head and knocking himself unconscious.

"Oh my God," my auntie exclaimed, rushing forward to check on him.

In my seven-year-old mind, my dad was my first knockout. And none more deserving.

Until I met David Evancho, my sophomore year of high school. He was totally mistreating his equally as popular and annoying girl-friend Cherie. But it wasn't my problem. Right up until he decided to make it the whole school's problem. Sending her nudes to the entire school over the public internet server. That man deserved a punch.

It didn't matter that his home life was only a step below mine. Instead, he was a two-headed hydra, who thought with the mere flick of his wrist that he could make a woman do anything he wanted. And with his words, he could virtually annihilate all of her free will. Cherie was powerless to stop him, but I wasn't. His reputation was in my hands, as we circled each other in the student parking lot. The crowd chanted my last name as if I were the only one standing between right and utter chaos.

He threw the first punch and missed. I threw mine and broke his nose.

I had never seen my dad so happy as he picked me up after my suspension. But flying fists don't solve every problem. Just the problems that aren't worth solving.

Chapter 1

"Michelle, what do you think about before a fight?" A reporter asked, shoving a microphone in my face. My manager failed miserably at keeping a handful of the local media back.

"When I stepped in the ring, I'm sitting across from my murderer. She wants me dead, and I like me alive. I'm fighting to live. I'm fighting to win."

"You heard the lady. Step back. You need room to prepare for true greatness," Gideon spouted, like an Evangelical preacher.

Every time I stepped into this place they swarmed me like bees attracted to the queen. Except one wrong word would turn these stingers against me. So I was always glad when my trainer, Farmer, pushed me safely into my changing room. I wasn't surprised at all that my manager, Gideon Botile, had stayed outside the door to entertain the masses.

It irked me to no end when people tapped me on the back wanting me to wax poetic about rearranging women's faces. Money and fame were never acceptable answers. Except in my case, the truth was closer to what I use the money for and that was my family obligations. That answer was worse than the first one.

And unlike other opponents who traveled with an entourage. I needed my team to travel light. This wasn't no picnic. If anything I really was attending my funeral. So usually during these things it was just me, Farmer, and my cutman Keith.

It was only fitting that my career would begin or end here, in local 399. The place where I started my amateur boxing career. From the outside, it looks like a fancy real estate office. However, the inside was all brawn. A permanent layer of dust on the floor from construction workers coming and going. It was so thick it would give anyone asthma. But in here, the back room. The smell of blood, sweat, and hard work reigned. It was stifling, like tear gas.

My first time here, I was 19, and out of place in a preppy ponytail and skinny jeans. But this time the place was just as a part of me as my bone marrow. In the same way that I was a part of it because of all my spent tears and strength. I was in the thick of it and coming out fine like the hulk. Local 399 had since upgraded some of its creature comforts. I like to think it was because of the money my shows were bringing in. One of the few things I had to be proud of. This changing room was state-of-the-art luxury.

But boxing wasn't my main priority. My son Owen was and he was at school waiting for me to make an appearance. After changing into my long red shorts that fell to my knees, and a simple white tank top, I hopped on top of my table.

"Farmer, don't let me forget to go to my son's debate tonight. It's his first one," I said to my trainer as he wrapped my hands with boxing tape.

"You just focus on the fight ahead."

I shouldn't have expected anything else from Farmer. He was like a father to me. Not that my real father was dead. He was most likely in V.I.P. enjoying the spoils with my boyfriend and champ, Darren Taylor. His last, but most recent fight, would ensure that he would have his own paparazzi snapping photos of him and his entourage. I would be surprised if my father wasn't hugged up with him in every one of those photos. He was never backstage with me helping me get ready, but he was the loudest man in the place.

It wouldn't usually bother me, but today I had made a promise to be at Owen's first debate. I didn't want to let him down. This fight would only typically last 15 minutes, so that wasn't the problem. I still had to go home, shower, ice my wounds, and change before hustling out the door. Just so that I could look like a regular PTA parent, but it was worth it for Owen.

"I'm as ready for this fight as I'll ever be. No contest. But I got shit to do. We just need to go."

"Cool it, Michelle," Farmer spouted tugging some red boxing gloves onto my hands. Farmer was about the same age as my father at 52, but their countenance was like night and day. It was the only reason I heeded his command. Smiling up at his rapidly growing grey beard and wondering how many of those hairs had my name on it. His brown syrupy eyes were stoic and serious. He tapped the gloves as a signal for me to test them before adding, "But yes, I'll remind you."

He hit my hands together and tested out the fitting of the gloves. I hopped down from the table and threw some jabs at Keith, who was holding up some boxing mitts. He had on a t-shirt with the name of our gym, Ever Fit, in the corner in red lettering. The noisiness from the hallway drifted into the small room as the door opened and Gideon entered.

"This is the first match of the rest of your life, and there's only six more after this before you're wearing the championship belt," he told me, sounding positively giddy. Or as giddy as greedy could sound.

I forced my concerns about making it to Owen's event out of my mind and focused on the fight ahead. My jet-black hair was already pulled back into a ponytail. The tail breaded.

"She's got the best team backing me. All she needs now is to concentrate on her elbow parry." The force behind Farmer's words alerted me to the fact that Gideon wasn't the only one looking for a guaranteed win tonight.

Gideon just grinned. "You're going to make us a lot of money, Michelle. Don't forget to get out there and smile for the cameras. Sell yourself."

I beckoned for Keith to put some headphones on my ears. Farmer came up behind me to help me into my red Ever Fit robe. I bounced up and down in place to get my heart rate up. Transitioning into the mindset of a killer. Walking out with my team behind me, listening to, Wanted Dead or Alive by Bon Jovi.

Pausing as I caught sight of my dad off to the side in the strands. He leaned over the barrier and yelled over the chaos. A beer in his hand. "Hit her like a man."

I laughed and returned the headphones to my head. With or without the headphones, I felt the audience's energy in my blood. Their faces were angry and teeming with unmet expectations. My gaze trained on the loser in the ring. Her hair was braided in cornrows as she hopped around in white shorts. Let's see how much blood I could get on them.

The crowd was in an uproar by the time I entered the ring. They were all die-hard fans who knew how this would end. There was no need to pay attention to the announcer rattling off my opponent's attributes when they could chant, second to none. Hightailing it out of the way to make room for the referee who demanded a false showing of showmanship.

A sugar high of kool-aid proportions hit me as soon as the bell rang. My training was like second nature. An easy one, two, three. This woman was still calculating her moves like an overdue homework assignment. Fighting wasn't just about skill though. It was equally about talent. And this woman was fighting scared.

I came out of the corner, bobbing and weaving. Leading with a flurry of straights with my left hand. I favor my right, but Keith has been having me practice more with the left. Just so I could throw off an unsuspecting opponent and it definitely showed in her eyes. Panic was taking hold. She decided to counter my attacks with a flurry of her own. None of which landed.

The trick to any bout, no matter the round, was not to act like I had already won. Even if it was clear that I had. Every underdog was that serial killer in the bushes waiting to catch me unaware. In Farmer's words, every fight should be fought as if it were still round one.

No one becomes "second to none" by skating by. I fight for that title every second. Which is why when the fifth and final bell rang, she wasn't my opponent anymore, but the grim reaper. Skeletal fingers that with a single touch would send me to the great beyond.

I couldn't let her touch me. Farmer pointed out to me that her hits were wild and unfocused. I used that to my advantage. My jabs sent her retreating into the corner, giving me the courage to lay into her. Pure white lightning that would send the grim reaper into hiding. Only to have the referee break up my onslaught.

I'm almost positive that she's feeling the pain. She doesn't get off another shot the whole round. Stumbling to the point that it would be easy to knock her down. But they don't give out points for mercy. So I throw a one-two combo and send her kissing the mat. She gets up at the count of five, but the bout is over. We go to our neutral corners, where Keith was waiting to fix me up.

The announcer eventually came and stood in the middle of the ring and announced, "Michelle "second to none" Nunn is the winner by unanimous decision."

I stood up and the referee sauntered over and held up my hand. Pleasantly surprised, when my opponent came over to shake my hand without any fanfare.

My friend and the only other woman under Gideon's roster Brooke Bowe stood on the corner ropes and waved and whistled. The only woman I knew that I could commiserate with on the harshness of the industry. She also sported a scary straight shot, displaying a power that even I dreaded going up against. But thanks to Gideon's maneuvering, all we were able to be was each other's biggest fans instead of rivals. I kissed two fingers and flashed them at her. Appreciating the love.

My least favorite part of winning was the media. The crowd's loud whistling almost drowned out their questions. Questions they demanded even if my body was falling apart. Farmer helped me into my robe. His arm lingered around my waist, and I mouthed thank you. Leaning all my weight against him. The fact that he knew I needed strength right now was why I respected him.

Gideon was oblivious, standing to my right, already plugging the next fight. However, the attention of most reporters was short and they were already on to a better story. So they needed to get through this quickly. After all, it was a Friday night in Chicago.

"Michelle, Michelle, what are your thoughts on the match?" The lone reporter who hadn't left asked, directing the attention away from Gideon.

"All the fools who didn't think I was a contender, start worrying!" I tasted the blood from my busted lip and spit it out unceremoniously on the mat.

Making my way through the condensed crowd to my boyfriend who was entertaining some reporters about his win. Half of them were supposed to be here for me. How could I not be angry that even my win was about him? Like clockwork, he saw me and the sea parted for him. Until he stopped and lifted me into the air, spinning me around. None of which was doing my headaches any favor.

"My baby's a winner just like me."

I tapped him lightly on the shoulder and signaled for him to put me down. Grinning through the aches and pains as he planted a kiss on my cheek. The whole world watching. "It's undeniable that we're winners. And I'll be the champion next."

Before we said anything else, Gideon stepped in to put in the final word. Like a wallpaper backdrop, I smooched Darren on the lips. Smiling at the flashing lights as we parted.

"You did good kid. Next time go for the KO," my dad said, pulling me into a surprising hug. His dirty gray hair was like popcorn balls on his scalp. A permanent tan from so many years working outside without sunscreen. He only stepped aside to allow Keith to hand me a towel. After he freed me from my boxing gloves, I wiped my mouth and soaked up some of the sweat pooling on the back of my neck.

"Let's get out of here," Darren whispered into my ear. His arm went around my shoulder, but instead of feeling loved, I felt bought and sold.

Quietly allowing him to lead us out of the ring. He pulled open the second and top rope to allow me through. Yet, he managed to lead the charge with my dad in front. I just shook my head and used the moment to interact with some of the fans in the stands. Shaking hands with as many as I could as we made our way back to the changing room.

Feeling crazy for noticing two hot guys at the end of the rows. One was a preppy looking blond, but the other was a tall glass of dark and handsome. I tried to chastise myself for even noticing. Chalking it up to my hormones escaping me.

Darren was twice as sexy as either of them. He even made the cover of GQ twice. A natural blond with the body of a sculpted Zeus. If any woman were to claim that he wasn't her type, I'd be inclined to think her crazy. Then again, maybe she just knew Darren as well as I did.

It occurred to me that some light flirting might actually throw Darren for a loop. I stopped and handed a tall dark and dazzling man my towel. "Keep it. You're going to want something of the future women's champion."

He looked surprised but took the towel. His warm fingers brushed across mine. I'm instantly rewarded with a warm smile that reached his amber eyes. He appeared to be around the same age as me and apparently was a huge fan of boxing. We already had nothing in common.

"We got to go," Farmer said from behind me.

I nodded to the two gentlemen and continued on. Stopping when I heard the end of the friend's conversation.

"...women's boxing is complete crap."

"What did you say?" I asked storming back.

It was like he reached into my chest and pulled out my heart. So I pulled back my right hand and punched Mr. Dark and Dazzling in the face. My fist connected with his jaw. It was Keith who pulled me back. Farmer giving me his best, what the fuck look. I merely turned to Gideon and said, "How is that for some personality?"

The guy held up his nose. "I think I'm bleeding?"

Chapter 2

I stormed off and ducked into the women's bathroom before anyone could grab me. Hiding behind the first stall I came too, willing myself not to cry. Locking it, I sat on the toilet as I rocked back and forth. This was not my world. Just because I had mastered the devil's den didn't mean that I didn't strive for Heaven. The hood of my silk robe was pulled down over my head. Crying into my aching and bruised hands. Only to choke on the sobs when I hear the door opening.

"You're an idiot," Farmer's voice echoed off the walls of the bathroom like an announcer in the ring. I could hear his hard strides across the floor. Smacking my lips, as I braced my foot against the door so he wouldn't open it. He tried to push on it, but I pushed back. Exhaling loudly, he gave up and walked back towards the sink.

"This is the woman's bathroom."

"I noticed. Just like I noticed that you ain't pissin' right now. What's going through your head hittin' that guy?"

I wasn't in the mood to answer any of my trainer's questions. Even though he was like a family member to me. The only person in the gym that I wished was my real father. Only to feel guilty because it wasn't like mines was dead. I knew he felt the same way about me though. He wasn't allowed to see his real daughter. Apparently, his wife was some socialite who had allowed her mother to come between them resulting in their divorce. A man who trained boxers to be violent wasn't safe around a kid either. So he rarely saw his daughter. That's why I didn't put up a fuss when Gideon assigned him as my trainer. Boxing took my free will and it took his marriage. We understood each other better than anyone.

Knowing that he was also Gideon's right hand, it was easy enough to figure out where he stood on this issue. That man only cared about money and I put us in a position to have that trifled with. So now Farmer was supposed to get me nice and softened up to kiss ass. But I needed him more and it was starting to make me bitter.

My back stiffened as I grit my teeth. "I'm guessing that Gideon's pissed?"

Not bothering to look between the crack in the door and the stall out of fear of what I'd see. Staring at the paint peeling on the corner of the door. Except for this small little infraction, this was the cleanest part of the whole building. Indicating that they didn't get a whole lot of women in this place.

"What do you think? You know what it's going to take to get this to go away?"

I actually didn't. My father didn't allow me to know the ends and outs of what makes this all run. Just enough to sign the contracts and make sure that the right amount of money is rolling in. There was no reason to push it. After all, I only needed to think of my son to remember that we need money.

"This goes beyond a simple fine by the World Boxing Association. Gideon's going to have to pull in some favors not to get you arrested and potentially banned. You know what that's going to cost?"

"So this asshole gets to pretend like he can whup my ass and the women's league is shit." I kicked the closed door for emphasis. "I taught him a lesson he needed."

I was only getting angrier despite knowing the truth behind his words. My father wasn't able to hide the rumors about Gideon beating people up and threatening other's family members. The man's reputation preceded him. He did whatever he had to in order to get his way. But my father's advice always played in my head. My job was to make sure that none of that wind was headed in the direction of me or my son. Everybody else wasn't my business. I was just supposed to stand upstream from the flame. It was the only good advice dad ever gave me.

However, it dawned on me that standing upstream didn't mean throwing down debris for others to catch. My guilty conscious reminded me that Dark, Dazzling, and Douche wasn't a part of this world and didn't need to be exposed to it through a punch in the face. Not that it was an excuse either. Some secretary behind a desk was going to have to lose my paperwork for the fine because she was worried about picking up her kid and him being missing. Or maybe some CEO would buy my head in order to keep me in boxing. I would be working for these people until they spent every drop of blood in my body to make up for it. Farmer was right, I should know better.

"This ain't just about Gideon, kid. I want to hear from you. What happened?"

I eased my foot off the door. There was no way that I was going to tell him that hearing those words hurt my feelings like a little baby. Even if they had. Farmer wasn't teaching no baby.

He sighed heavily, accepting my silence as defeat. "Don't worry about Gideon or that guy. These things work themselves out. You just take a breath and calm down. Don't hit anyone on the way back to the room."

Smirking, I get up and unlock the door. "Can we at least agree he deserved it?"

But he didn't hear me. The door swung silently in his absence. I walked up to the mirror and splashed some water on my face. Drying off with a harsh brown paper towel. Before taking down my hair. "He was just a jerk. What he said about your profession doesn't matter? You're Michelle Nunn. Your skill is second to no one. Don't be in a bathroom crying like a baby. You got this."

I didn't show my face in that changing room until I got it together. Only to walk in on Gideon laughing his ass off with my father. I'm glad someone was having fun. My whole body was aching after that fight and I was emotionally spent. Gideon and Farmer were in another corner with their heads together.

"I better go make sure that guy isn't going to sue. I'd say that you were wrong, but you can't buy that kind of publicity," Gideon said, turning to leave.

I wondered if that meant Farmer was wrong and he wasn't angry. Maybe no one would have to pay for my slip. Except for Dark, Dazzling, and Douche and he deserved it. A nasty personality can sometimes make you look ugly. No one was allowed to disrespect the hard work that I put into my craft, but me. Yet Farmer's pensive gaze sent me crashing back to reality. Checking me with his gaze.

I groaned, trying to keep it cool as regret really set in. My son should always be my first thought so hitting that douche was still a mistake. With or without the strong hand of Gideon crashing down. A night in jail would be hard to explain to an impressionable eight-year-old. It wasn't exactly good role modeling either. I cocked my head at Farmer who clearly wanted to say something. "Just go ahead and say it."

"Since when did you become so damn sensitive? What changed?"

What if I wasn't even sure.

Smiling a cheeky half-grin, Darren grabbed me around the waist and pulled me towards him. Playing it up for our audience. "That was just a little pint-up aggression. People better be ready for my baby and move the hell out of the way."

"Yeah, that's nothing new. My daughter knows how to bring down the hammer."

Darren nuzzled my neck and my hand went instinctively around his head to tangle in his hair. Feeling a tad exposed, with my father in the room. All he needed to see was that we were the perfect couple. I didn't want to go too far.

"Will talk about this later," Farmer quipped. "Get to your kid's event."

Keith followed him out the door, leaving me alone with Darren and my dad. I turned and gripped the dark grey fur lining of Darren's leather jacket. Ready to throw out a lifeline for him to take. He just had to grasp it.

"Yeah, good reminder. My son's debate is tonight. Will you come with me?"

"Baby, I'm going to the after-party tonight. Somebody got to celebrate this win of yours." He grinned. "I'm your representative, remember."

Another missed shot. I shouldn't be disappointed, but I am. My heart shouldn't crumble, but it is. It's like throwing a fight, you know you're supposed to lose and still being upset about it. I turned in his arms to ask my father. "How about it dad? Give me a ride?"

He frowned as if he were upset that I even asked. "I was going with Darren. Sweetie, you should have told me this sooner."

"Yeah, I guess I should've." It didn't seem worth it to fight over the fact that I had told him two weeks ago.

Darren tapped me on the ass and got up. Halfway to the door before I could blink. "James, we've got a car waiting."

"I'll catch up," my dad replied.

I lifted myself onto the table. Quickly throwing off my shoes and socks, I replaced them with fresh ones. But I hated it the most when my toes felt icky. Slowly unwrapping my hands next. My knuckles were bleeding from the scrape with the guy's face. I flexed them to get some of the movement flowing so they wouldn't stiffen up. Worried about how I was going to get back to my house when Darren was my ride. Looking up into my dad's eyes, as he approached me. "Enjoyed the fight?"

His grin widened, delight lighting up his face. "That fire you displayed after the brawl is exactly what's going to make us millions when you finally step in the ring with the reigning champ. But you need to make better choices."

"Come on dad," I groaned, looking away.

He grabbed my chin and forced me to look at him. His thumb and forefinger practically indented into my jaw. It didn't matter that I was almost 29. Instantly, I started shaking. Swallowing hard as I waited for the punch that would never come. He hasn't hit me since I was 18, but my insides still shrank inside whenever he touched me like frostbite.

"You'll be fightin' behind bars for free you keep entertaining trust fund babies."

"I know dad," I said, through gritted teeth.

"This ain't high school. Keep your hands to yourself or I'll break them myself. I'm not going to let you ruin this opportunity for us."

"I got it."

He relinquished my head, but in a way that caused a sharp shooting pain as my neck snapped back. Eyeing me a moment longer before he said, "You good? Nobody checked you out."

"I'm fine."

My gaze never left my hands.

"Don't blow up that man's phone tonight either. Will be out late. He doesn't need stress from you."

"Dad, when have I ever done that?" I asked getting really tired. Darren and I didn't have that type of relationship. No matter how I may wish it was different. In dads mind, I was just like every woman he had ever dated. He had to protect his favorite son-in-law from my feminine crazy. Even if it didn't exist.

"Tell my grandson, I love him."

"Of course." Just glad when he finally left. Tears welling up in my eyes. I always had to think about my career first. No questions asked.

Chapter 3

My plans always have to include a mad dash through the subway. Or a last-minute cab ride. If I was going to get anywhere on time. However, Owen's event tonight called for all the stops. So that meant calling for a cab. I still needed to stop off at home to freshen up and change.

My knuckles were still bleeding from the scrape with the guy's face. So I could imagine what the rest of me looked like. I flexed my hand to get some movement flowing. So they wouldn't stiffen up on me. Paying the cab driver extra to wait. As I ran upstairs to get into the shower. Throwing off my clothes with manic precision.

We lived on the third floor of a brownstone. The first thing I got after I won my first match. It was a bigger two-bedroom apartment for my son and I. He was only one at the time. But for me, it was like purchasing my first castle. One where Owen would have his own room. The kitchen and dining room were small and we had to share a bathroom, but it was still magical to me.

After hopping out of a shower, that my body badly needed to soak in, I washed my face. I gently applied my makeup to bring some color back into my face and hide the bruises. A huge red and black bruise on my left cheekbone. Opting for a nude lipstick to hide the bruise on my lip. I hoped Owen appreciated all of this effort.

Throwing on a simplistic floral print, navy blue dress that would surely please the adults at this thing. I looked down at my watch and realized that it had already been an hour. The event started at eight and it was already nine. This prompted me to grab my purse and fly out the door to the cab, I had waiting.

Shaking my head as I threw open the door and hopped in. "Sorry about all this."

He merely shrugged. "It's your dollar."

Nothing was too high a price to pay when it comes to my son. Watching the street lights fly by as he weaved in and out of traffic. My heart was tap dancing down Lake Shore Drive, the closer we got to his elementary school. Everyone in that place made me feel so inadequate. As if I were a walking billboard for violence and the far reach of toxic masculinity. How would any of them be able to understand that I was just me? Sort of.

I paid the cab driver and stepped out in front of the school. A well-manicured, and up-to-date, red brick building. Hoping, that the parents coming out with their kids didn't mean what I thought. I tried to keep my head held high as if I weren't some vagrant, but another parent wanting to cheer on her son. My head told me that no manner of perfume and showers could ever make me a normal parent.

Once inside, my steps faltered as soon as I saw two of my favorite people standing outside the auditorium. Owen saw me first and barely acknowledged my presence. But my auntie Shannon waved me over to where she was talking to a teacher. One that I hadn't remembered meeting. Owen fidgeted uncomfortably in the grey suit

I had bought him. Tugging on his shirt collar and scratching his pants leg.

"You did great, Owen," the woman stated quickly, before sauntering past me. Not bothering to introduce herself. She barely managed a thin-lipped smile. I may not have heard of her, but my reputation certainly preceded me. One more person that I had to make an effort with to bridge the gap in this building.

"That was Owen's debate teacher, Mrs. Coyne. She also teaches sixth grade," my auntie said, filling me in.

My aunt was closer to 60 but looked 30 in her pink pencil skirt suit. Her blond hair fell loosely around her shoulders. Like faded gold that lost its luster, but not its beauty. But more importantly, I could always count on her to come through for Owen. Unlike my father.

I turned to Owen, who still hadn't said anything. "I'm here, baby. I know I'm late, but I'm here. That's got to count for something?"

"No, it doesn't."

He stomped past me, pouting. I looked back at my aunt who was just staring. "I fucked up...again. I knowwww."

"Actually I was just wondering...well, you're wearing a dress."

I didn't know whether to curtsy or bow. "I thought I should get one for occasions like these."

She looked astonished. "You look beautiful."

I ignored the compliment and followed the direction that Owen had gone. "So how bad is it?

"He lost, but I don't think that's why he's giving you the cold shoulder. Owen's next debate is after your fifth fight. Put it in your phone so you don't forget. The rest will work itself out."

I blinked back tears of frustration.

"God auntie, I had a match. And then I still had to make it home and fix this," I said gesturing to my body. "Even if I had come straight here after the fight, I would have looked like I'd been assaulted."

She grabbed my hand. "You don't have to explain anything to me." She nodded to the double doors where Owen was waiting. "Explain it to him. All little boys want is their momma." She relinquished my hand and rubbed my back. "Especially one as kickass as you."

I came up behind Owen and enveloped him in a hug. Kissing the top of his head. His thick auburn hair reminded me of his father. "Come on. Auntie's going to give us a ride home. You can get ready for bed and fill me in on everything I missed."

He pushed open the doors and yanked away from my embrace. "What's the point?"

"Let him be angry for a little while. It's okay," my auntie said, following up behind him.

I just shook my head, unsure of how to respond to his reaction. It was times like these that made me wish that he had two parental figures in his life. Not a deadbeat gym rat of a father who had delusions of grandeur of the Olympic type. That conveniently led him away from any genuine responsibility.

On the car ride home, Owen fell asleep in the backseat. Without my auntie here, I'd probably be falling apart right now. I just wished that my drink-loving, party-obsessed father was just as interested in his grandson. The only thing he loved was my popular boxer boyfriend, Darren.

"How was the fight?"

"It was okay."

I thought about telling her about the guy I hit and everything that came after. However, my father's words haunted me as if he were right beside me hindering my movements. And I wasn't a little kid anymore, she couldn't rescue me from him. If she ever could.

He approached me after the room had emptied out. Pretending to want to discuss the fight.

"That fight you displayed after the brawl is exactly what's going to make us millions when you finally step in the ring with the reigning champ. But you need to make better choices."

"Come on dad," I groaned, looking away.

He grabbed my chin and forced me to look at him. His thumb and forefinger practically indented into my jaw. It didn't matter that I was almost 29, my heart instantly plummeted. Swallowing hard as I waited for the punch that would never come. He hadn't hit me since I was 18. Yet my innards still shrank inside whenever he touched me like frostbite.

"You'll be fightin' behind bars for free you keep entertaining trust fund babies."

"I know dad," I said through gritted teeth.

"This ain't high school. Keep your hands to yourself or I'll break them myself. You're not going to ruin this."

"I get it."

He relinquished my head, but in a way that caused a sharp shooting pain when my neck snapped back. Eyeing me a moment longer before he said, "You good? Nobody checked you out."

"I'm fine."

My gaze never left my hands. Just happy when he finally left. I always had to think about my career first. No questions asked. Even on the car ride home from my son's event.

She parked and I got Owen upstairs and put him to bed. Thanking my lucky stars that tomorrow was Saturday. I ventured into the kitchen and got out a healthy snack I made of, beef jerky trail mix. Only to come out to the living room to see my aunt watching the news. I was about to kick this young woman out to enjoy the rest of her evening when I caught sight of the guy I hit on the news. My eyes bugged out of my head.

Cognizant, of not wanting to wake Owen. I turned the volume up a little and stretched the tight muscles in my neck as I prepared for the obvious BS about to fall.

"So what happened tonight?" the female reporter asked. The only reporter who hadn't abandoned me for Darren.

"It was my buddy's first time at a women's boxing match. I was a huge fan, and he's kind of the skeptic," the blond-haired guy began, pronouncing every word like a man born of pedigree. Taking charge of the interview as if he were the important one. The actual injured one stood stoically by his side.

"Why? Don't tell me that you're one of those guys who believe women can't box because we have babies," she jokingly asked. But with the way she shoved that mic in the friend's face it was no joke.

"Obviously not. Boxing is boxing," he said, sounding nasally with tissue stuffed up his nose.

"He does," my aunt and I said simultaneously. I propped my feet up on the coffee table. My gaze fluttered over my gray toenail polish. As I leaned my head back on the brown upholstered couch.

"I've followed the sport for a very long time," the blond guy piped in, clearly enjoying the camera. "Michelle Nunn is one of the best. As is her boyfriend, who's also a formidable boxer. Tonight, her opponent wasn't fully prepared for everything that Michelle was offering up. And it was clear to anyone in the stands why we now call her second to none."

"Okay guys, so what went wrong?"

"She was greeting fans, shaking hands. And she got to us and handed Mark her towel. The only words that were exchanged were from her and it was just a show of bravado. I'm a winner type deal."

My aunt looked over at me and grinned mischievously. "You certainly left some things out of your, okay, response."

I rolled my eyes. "Owen was with us."

She looked back towards the bedroom as if she had forgotten that he was even there. But I had been eyeing the hallway every 60 seconds to ensure that he didn't wake up and come out here.

"When she walked away, I said something to Mark like, do you still think woman's boxing is crap?"

"I wasn't sold. I said it was still crap and she heard me and decked me."

An ambulance could be seen in the background like a glaring omission to my stupidity. I was embarrassed that my son could have seen this. We even had matching bruises. Although, his was smaller and much more inconspicuous. Mark was clearly an idiot, but he wasn't worth the trouble I would have gotten into. Why was it so hard for me to think first before reacting?

Maybe it was my hormones that got me so distracted. High off adrenaline and a fresh win. You can sometimes feel a little frisky. There was no putting out that fire with Darren. So a hot guy in the crowd was my only outlet. For a second I was just a teen with a crush. Instead of a badass with a kid and enough sense to know better. I was not this guy's type and wouldn't want to be.

"Are you going to sue or press charges?" The reporter asked.

I chewed on the bottom of my lip anxiously, accidentally nipping at my busted lip, drawing blood.

"No. I'm a converted believer now. I think her manager is going to send me her autograph and some promo tickets. That's good enough."

I raised my eyebrow. At first, I was hearing of it, but it made sense. Gideon was a man of his word. Certainly was the least I could do for him not pressing charges.

"Well, that's awesome that there are no hard feelings." She pushed the mic toward the blond guy. "You think you're friend is done underestimating—-"

"The next..."

Auntie Shannon reached for the remote and turned the television off. "I'm going to come right out and say it. I'm concerned. The Michelle I know isn't going to go all Tyson on a fan."

"I don't need to be psychoanalyzed," I said gruffly, standing up. "This is the only thing I'm good at." Shaking my fist at the television like an old woman. "Some pretty boys don't get to decide that it's meaningless. I do enough of that on my own."

"Awww baby." She smacked her lips and got up to give me a hug.

Training was my life. Leaving me to fail at everything, but the one thing I don't want. My father's dream.

Chapter 4

It was Saturday and Owen had already decided to spend it freezing me out. He obviously hadn't gotten over my parenting fail last night. The only thing I could get out of him this morning was what kind of cereal he wanted. I needed to be home with him today. But I was also talking contracts and my dad would filet me alive if I didn't go today. The only good thing was that Gideon had a hard and fast rule that I always watch the taped fights the next day. It gave me an unofficial day off from the grind.

"I hope you aren't as rude to your auntie as you are to me," I stated flatly, picking up Owen's empty cereal bowl and carrying it into the kitchen. In nothing more than a sports bra and yoga pants. "Maybe we can watch a movie together tonight?"

"Why? I'll only end up watching it with Auntie."

I stormed back into the living room and grabbed him. Getting down to his level. "I think about you all the time, and I'll always be here for you. Even when I'm not good at it. But I'll try because I love you." He struggled against my cuddles as I pulled him onto the couch. "You're my little purple goober. You'll always be more important than anything else."

He looked up at me, touching my cheek lightly. "Does it hurt?"

"It's healing. That's never a painless process."

"I don't understand. Why do you do it, if it hurts so much? Didn't you want to be something else growing up? Auntie Shannon says I can be whatever I want to be when I grow up. So I decided to be a doctor. That way I can fix you when you get home from your fights."

"That's sweet, baby. I'm sure you'll be a great doctor and I'll be your first patient. But I box to keep food on the table." I rubbed the top of his head. "But I was little like you once. I used to want to be a dancer. Grandpa James, helped me realize that my dream wasn't very practical. And I needed something really special to take care of you. I'd never regret that."

Someone knocked on the door and I moved to answer it.

"Will you ever go back to your dreams?" he asked, already becoming distracted by the cartoons that he put on the TV screen.

Taking off the deadbolt, I replied simply, "I've got different dreams now."

It was Auntie Shannon. "I know you're only here to babysit, but could you do a load of laundry? I'm running out of socks."

She threw her head back and laughed. "You're such a weirdo, but yes. And let's stop talking about that because I've got updates."

I bit the inside of my cheek. "Owen, go watch those cartoons in your room, please."

She waited until he was gone before saying anything else. "The whole world knows about your temper. At least they've decided that you have one."

I eyed my auntie wearily as she went to sit on the couch. She looked gorgeous even while delivering bad news. It was hard not to be jealous of her fashion sense. My father had crippled mine. Yet, here she sat with a pale pink leather jacket on and a pair of grey jeans and a matching shirt. In any store, I would find myself floundering.

"Variations of that interview have been playing all day on the news. As well as video of you actually hitting him."

"Okay, that's kind of bad," I said going to the closet and pulling out my gym shoes. A clean pair of socks was already tucked inside.

"Not all the opinions voiced were good."

I pulled on my plain ankle socks, followed by my black and purple gym shoes. "I'll be okay."

I grabbed my light blue windbreaker and headed down the stairs. Texting Farmer at the bottom.

Michelle: I'm on my way.

He texted back quickly.

Farmer: Sorry we moved. I'll text you the new address.

I read the text in disbelief. "When did we move?"

An hour later, and one simple subway ride, I was standing in front of a beautiful building that looked like it once belonged to a restaurant. Sporting wood trim and beige staccato with brick accents. But the name on the front said Center Stage Dance Studio. Five-year-old me wanted to do the jitterbug. But adult me knew that public transportation had never been my best subject in Chicago Citizen 101. So it was a possibility that I was lost. However, the address on my phone that matched the one on the building would clearly refute that.

"Okay, listen," Farmer said flying out of the building. "I know we share everything. Don't freak out."

I put my phone away and pointed to the door. "You just came out of a dance studio. I'm a little freaked."

"Gideon lost his health insurance at the River North location. So they shut him down. I had to think on my feet."

I frowned. "How is this dance studio supposed to help?"

"I'm letting everyone use my gym temporarily."

He would always be a foreman to me. It was hard for me to see him with his own gym. "You own a whole gym, inside a dance studio?"

He ran his hands through his hair, clearly frustrated. But I was growing angry with his rushed explanations.

"Yes and No. My ex-wife owns it. It's actually in the basement of this place." He clapped his hand on my shoulder. "Please, don't be angry with me. This place was a part of my forgotten past. If I was hiding it from anyone it was Gideon, not you."

I looked skyward, holding onto my temper as it threatened to swallow me. Looking back at him when I was much calmer. "Do I get to meet the infamous ex-wife now?"

"You don't want to swim in the deep end of my dysfunctional life when you got one of your own. Gideon and your father are waiting for you." He threw his arm around my shoulders. "Here let's sign in at reception first."

This place had a reception? Gideon's gym had a long winding staircase with one light. No one would willingly go down those steps unless they belonged there. But I plastered on a smile. Not wanting to disappoint him by showing my unease.

The place was bright and airy with modern touches. Paintings of dancers in large distressed white frames on the wall. Two large chandeliers hanging from the ceiling above the reception desk. It felt like I really was lost only to end up in the VIP section of heaven. Any moment now, I was going to be escorted out.

Farmer grinned as he handed me a fancy turquoise clipboard. That looked like it folded in half. The top of which had the name of the gym, Ever Fit, printed out in fancy cursive lettering. I forced a smile as I signed my name. Would it be against the rules to kick down the door of the old gym and return there? I handed her back the clipboard and followed Farmer.

"Mark will be in later and we don't want to be empty-handed. There are some memorabilia down here for you to sign. And practice being charming," he said, leading me down some well-lit steps. "Just in case you have to kiss a little ass."

I grinned. "You saying, I'm not charming."

"I'm pretty sure you run on Gatorade, brawls, and cuss words. So no."

We made it downstairs and I barely had time to look around before my phone was blowing up. I picked it up immediately, my thoughts going to my son. "Hello."

"That's a pretty Tragus earring, but I'm more interested in your face."

My eyebrows shoot up as I realized that voice was Darren's and not my aunt's. Causing me to quickly pull the phone away from my ear.

"It's your day off. Come hang with me?"

I stared down at the floor. "Darren, what's this about? I'm spending time with Owen—"

"Hold up. Turn your head. How's your face coming along?" He asked, leaning into his phone.

"It's healing," I replied, doing as I was told.

"Naw, on second thought, scratch that. You will be out here looking like I beat you. Just meet me at my house. You can hang out with Owen after."

I took a deep breath, looking up at Farmer through my eyelashes who was politely pretending not to listen. "You can't just hijack my time."

"It's just lunch," he said rubbing his nose, before clicking off. A signal that there would be photographers there to take some "accidental" photos of us.

"Turd." Farmer faked coughed into his hand.

Tongue in cheek, I stared him down, practically threatening him to keep it up. Farmer was of the impression that I deserved more. So was I, but in boxing, there was more at play than just the game. Just like there was more to war than just the fighting. "Where's my work?"

He walked over to a small table and picked up some photos and a set of pink boxing gloves. Shoving them into my arms, before plopping a huge black marker on top. "Mark is awesome by the way."

"Not yesterday."

He just shook his head and pointed to an office across the room. "They're waiting for you in there."

I walked past a ring that looked like it was covered in a layer of dust from non-use. A small black couch was shoved against a gray cement wall opposite it. They had a lot of work to do if this was going to be the new base of operations. There wasn't even any workout gear. The cobwebs still needed to be dusted from the corners. But I loved it. Only because I just knew I'd get a few more days off.

Gideon was already sitting at a desk fit for a king in a rather small office. I tried to imagine Farmer sitting in that same spot and couldn't. Of course, my father was sitting across from him. They both looked as thick as slick oil.

I sat down in the chair opposite my dad's and prayed that the lectures would be quick. Throwing myself into my work. So they'd think of me as the studious apologetic boxer they wanted me to be.

"Now, that you're in a signing mood. Here's the contract for the next bout." Handing over a single sheet of paper in a blue manila folder. It was the same standard language that I'd read in all of them. So I just went down the sheet initialing the rules and expectations.

"Initial manager shall be paid by the promoter."

I looked up, my hand hovering above the section. It was standard for me to pay him out of my purse. He always drummed into my head that it was the only way for me to ensure that he always got paid. "You sure?"

"I trust this guy."

I signed my name and made my way down the sheet. It must've been an honor to count oneself as a part of Gideon's inner circle. He was a shrewd businessman that could never be seen out of a suit.

My first tryout to be his client was in the parking lot of a strip club. Anyone who hears this story usually laughs because my first opponent was a feisty stripper named Chocolate Summer. But she gave me the fight of my life. Gideon swore from that moment on that he only saw a winner in me. And in less than a year, with Farmer's help, he had me feeling like one. Five years later I'm in my prime.

I scrolled down to the end of the page. Quickly reviewing the money terms. "Only $750 for six rounds? But it's so quick. Only a week of prep time."

Gideon ran his hand along the scruff of his beard. "News promo wasn't a draw. In fact, it's been a liability. The owner wants no foolishness at his club. I'll try again later. *If* you win this next one."

He emphasized the word if like he doubted me. Normally, that would set me off but I could feel my father's gaze burrowing into me.

"There wont be any more incidents like the last one," he almost growled. "Michelle understands that we need another good fight to help people forget the last one."

"I'm a reformed woman." I placed the signed contract and promo pack back on Gideon's desk. He flipped through them quickly, giving his stamp of approval. An impressive David Yurman ring on his finger. The stone was as chaotic as his mind was.

"Let's watch the video," my father said, scooting to the edge of his chair.

An old tube TV on top of a very large black cart was wedged in the corner of the room. Gideon pressed play and leaned back in his chair, pulling out a Cuban cigar.

"So the blacks like the cigars too?" My dad asked unabashedly. A grin on his face.

Placing the cigar down, Gideon simply replied, "Some."

"That's cool."

The glare he was giving my dad could have sliced his kidneys open. But dad was oblivious. I shrunk down in my seat and wished that fighting gave me a voice. Instead of giving everyone but me one. Dad wouldn't even need to be here. My thoughts drifted to the main perpetrator, Darren. Farmer had no clue what the real arrangement was between me and Darren. All anyone needed to see was that we were the perfect couple. But behind closed doors, Darren was more like my representative than my boyfriend.

Our entire relationship was a farce. He's great to me in public and cheating in private. During a drunken rant, he even admitted to me that he was only with me to prop his image as a boxer. Truthfully, I needed the career boost too, but I got my self-respect. The only reason that I hadn't kicked him to the curb was because being together made my father happy. His happiness was my sadness. It was always that way with boxing.

Chapter 5

Getting injured during a fight is par for the course.

But a bitch is losing badly if they start bitin'.

"She bit me. She bit me," I stammered, breathing heavily as I sat in the corner.

"It's a foul. The ref caught it. I heard Burnside was getting cocky and sitting out on practices all week," Farmer barked into my ear. Reminding me that every fight was important even the second one.

Keith wiped at the sweat on my brow and poured antiseptic on the wound inflicted on my shoulder. It stung so bad that I pounded on the ropes. The woman's teeth marks were embedded in my skin like some new-age tattoo. Choosing the sixth round to turn into some rabid dog when she had already lost. I was just waiting for the judges to confirm the same thing. Staring at my opponent who sat across from me, I badly wished this was a street fight.

"Hey." A voice called out to me from behind.

I turned to see Farmer hopping down in order to give Gideon some room.

"You did good, fighter."

I simply nodded. My whole body was sore as it came to life. Surveying the crowd with new eyes. "This place is packed."

"Guess you didn't scare everyone away after all."

"I want double next fight."

The announcer moved to the center of the ring and I stood up. Eyeing my opponent wearily. The woman was clearly physically and mentally weak. Resorting to tricks in order to make her way to the top.

"By unanimous decision, Michelle "second to none" Nunn is the reigning winner.

The crowd erupted into raucous applause. Bigger than any that I had heard before. Even booing when Kaia Burnside bit me. Did I finally have a rabid fan base? The spotlight moved throughout the crowd as my famous pro boxer boyfriend, Darren "Ironclad" Botile, made his way to the ring. Of course, the announcer chose then to shove the microphone in my face. I just grinned, "I really ain't got nothing to say. I love you all for the support. And no hard feelings to Kaia. I know I taste like Churros. I'm just irresistibly delicious."

But Darren must've felt the same way because he stayed with me even after everyone had left. Even reassuring me that everything was fine when my father didn't show up today. And he would give him a play-by-play of the bout later. This place had a shower and I wanted to feel less like a hobo before I went home to Owen.

Dressed and ready to go, he approached me and laid two kisses on my lips. The first was soft and quick as if he wasn't sure that he should do it. Its twin, hard and deepening, as if it derived from a hungry part of him.

Nothing but shocked, I pulled back. "Woah fella, what's going on?"

"I think our fierce chemistry demands that we start taking this relationship seriously. Come back to my place and celebrate with me?"

"That's sweet, but I'm——-."

"Going to be with Owen," he finished for me.

He looked so distraught it was throwing me a bit. What really was our relationship? A business deal. Something more casual or more than all of it. Earlier this week, Brooke brought over a box of paperwork from the old location. In it were tons of the envelopes and notes I had stuffed in Darren's locker. Some were unopened, with birthday invitations and BBQ events. I was crashing and burning every time I offered up more serious options. "Maybe I could cook dinner for us after I put him to bed."

"Not much of a celebration."

"I guess...but..."

"Forget it. Maybe next time."

I watched flummoxed as he left me standing in the locker room alone. It was starting to feel like we were overdue for a heart-to-heart. And now he wasn't giving me a ride home either. That was the real Darren that I had grown to know and loathe. I gathered my backpack and made the slow trek to the train.

But by the time I had helped Owen with his homework and put him to bed. I was rethinking my decision. Feeling like a petulant teenager, I blurted out, "I want to go see Darren?"

What I was not expecting was for her to burst into laughter. Spasmed chuckles rippled through her body, bringing tears to her eyes. I sighed and looked away, feeling like an idiot. Only looking back when she stopped.

"Oh, you're serious. Why?" she asked grabbing my hands as if we had both attended an intervention.

"I think something deeper might be happening between us and I don't want to miss it."

She looked at me pityingly. "Did you get hit in the head today?"

I pulled my hands from her grasp. More than a little exasperated.

She pursed her lips. "Michelle, let's be serious. Your relationship with Darren is as deep as a kiddie pool. You know that. What's going on here?"

"We shared a moment...maybe."

"Don't let that heat between your legs get you in trouble. That man looks at you as nothing more than a meal," she held my chin, forcing me to look at her.

"I've got to make lemonade out of lemons at some point." Gently pushing her hand away.

"Or you could throw the whole drink away and leave him. You're a grown woman, Michelle. It's high time that you act like it. My brother-in-law can't tell you where to plant that flower between your legs."

None of her statements were new to me. I craved them like water. Yet words were different from actions. And my career wasn't just my father's concern. It was also keeping food on the table for Owen and me. Being the only thing that I was ever good at, it deserved the ironclad boost.

"Go. I'll spend the night."

I gave her a somber smile. "Thanks."

"Just don't get pregnant."

I rolled my eyes, practically jumping off the couch. "Fuck mom, really."

"Hold your tongue."

Even as I kissed my son goodnight and avoided my aunt's shameful gaze. I tried to ignore the nagging feeling that I was just kidding myself. Especially since the voice sounded like my aunts.

I remembered my first time in Darren's apartment. New to the game, he had come off as a celebrity in my young eyes. His loft-style living reminded me of the potential possibilities of my own situation. In that one day, he had been elevated to the status of Christian Grey and every boy band-er that I had ever pinned after. Little did I know then that he didn't typically date women in the industry. Yet, some of those butterflies were coming back as I tried to imagine the possibilities between us.

Since, my renewed success, I really hadn't been back to this place. I chose to focus on my career, rather than whether Darren had some lace panties hidden under the carpet. Yet the sheer lasciviousness of the lobby of the building made me wonder if these fights would one day pay for Owen's private school. Darren was certainly living the high life.

I took the elevator up to the penthouse. Fried nerves settled in like old nail polish. The hallway was suddenly freakishly long as I made my way to his apartment. Instead of the few short steps that it was. Knocking lightly as if I still had the choice to run when I was past that.

A woman in nothing but black underwear answered the door. Her creamy pale skin was as smooth as milk. Thankful that her long brown hair covered her bare breasts.

"Hey, you're that boxer that punched that guy. He deserved it. All men are dogs."

I raised a shocked eyebrow at her euphemism. "Are they now?"

"Totally."

"Whose at the door?" Darren asked, from somewhere inside.

"Your girlfriend. She's also as cool as you said," she replied, looking over her shoulder. "It's so cool that you two have this new-age relationship. I bet yours will outlast them all."

Her hair moved, revealing a peek of pink nips, and I quickly averted my eyes. Darren rushed to the door breathing heavily as if he had just run across the state.

To think I was going to trust this idiot with my heart. The fact that I had gotten it all wrong pissed me off more than the cheating. I still couldn't tell a jerk from a good guy. How was I supposed to trust myself to make good choices? It was now obvious that on top of being too trusting. I was also delusional.

"Go," he barked, fixing his pants and closing the door behind him.

I gazed into eyes full of sorrow and it made me want to rethink my hitting policy. He was a master manipulator. Even now he wanted me to somehow think he cared, that he had a heart in that empty shell of a body. But I knew better now.

"Michelle."

"We have an understanding." I should want to punch him in the face. But I don't. He clearly sent mixed signals. But I don't need to know why. Punching someone a second time would have gotten me a reputation. Not that I had the will to punch her. During my short two-minute conversation with Blue Lagoon, I came to an understanding all my own.

"Let me explain."

I don't want him to explain. It hurt enough that I was tied to him, but it would hurt more if he caste lies like bait to trick me.

I turned around and walked back to the elevator without another word. Throwing my arm in the air to wave away all the trouble.

"We have an understanding."

Chapter 6

I stood on the platform of the train trying to figure out if I should go right or left? The right was home to Shannon and Owen. Hours earlier than my aunt would be expecting and that would draw questions. The left was to the studio and gym and no one could be there. But I wouldn't get questions. So I went left.

Just like this whole thing with Darren went left. Maybe I craved love more than I didn't. I'm not just a fighting machine. Even though sometimes life makes me feel like that is all there is. I'm 28 with one kid, and no romantic prospects because the whole world thinks I'm taken.

I end up crying in front of Center Stage Dance Studio.

The source of my kiddie-sized delusions. Yet the only place where Farmer would be here to help me punch it out. I'd never admit this to even my aunt, but I think I want something serious. It's just not allowed.

I entered to find the reception desk empty. The place was dark except for a small light that peeked underneath the door of Studio 1. As gracefully as I could manage I snuck past the gym door. A new sign had been put on the door that read, Ever Fit. I tried the handle, but it was locked.

I wiped the tears from my cheeks and lightly slapped them to appear more lively. Peering down the hallway, my next option was to knock and ask if Farmer had returned after the fight. It was as simple as a yes or no and then I'd be out of their hair. I guess I'd rather bet on that than head home feeling like a lonely shrew.

Like The Queen in Snow White, I peered through the glass to see what I was getting myself into first. There were more chandeliers in this room. Except these looked like cheerleading pom poms. But when the guy turned around it was Mr. Dazzling and Douche himself. I nearly stopped breathing at the sight of Mark. This time he was dressed in a black button-up and black dress pants. I found myself licking my lips as I took him in fully.

He was no boy wonder. Hiding broad shoulders and a muscular build behind choir boy clothes. An untamed lion, perfectly anticipating his partner's next move. His eyes closed as if the music played behind his eyelids like a Broadway play.

I pressed my face against the window like a kid at the Zoo. It felt as if I was watching this intimate moment for only me to see. Growing envious that I had none of her beauty or even half of his talent. The little girl in me reminded me that I wanted to be her.

I didn't recognize his equally as hot dance partner. They looked beautiful together as they moved about the floor. My favorite part was not the lifts, but their distinct movements as one. Their movements were one after the other, in a way that a mistake would be obvious, but they're not making any. It was so amazing that I had to know what song they were playing. What classic symphony would allow them to tune out even each other and just dance like one? Curiosity prompted me to open the door.

Surprised when the song, Run to You, by Bryan Adams, reached out to me through my depressive fog.

Before I knew it I was dancing in front of the door. Whipping my head back and forth and swiveling my hips to the beat. Doing my best strip tease impression for an audience of none. Completely in my own little world until the song ended sending me crashing to Earth. Turning to stare into the agape gazes of the dancers. His girlfriend looked pissed, but Mark looked amused. I don't know if Farmer not being here or everything I'd been through tonight, but I needed that smile.

Despite his appealing and intense gaze, the angry daggers his girl-friend was shooting me reminded me to speed things up. I needed to get out of here.

"Let's try that again. The right away," Mark said walking up to me and holding out his hand.

I was just surprised that he hadn't wanted to berate me. Tentative-ly taking his hand as if it were an alligator and might snap at me. My hand in his wasn't as small and dainty as Caliece's. Neither were they manicured, the grey polish chipped and faded. Did male dancers care about that sort of thing? But the way he held my hand was the same as if it were fragile. And they molded together like it was the most natural thing in the world.

"Mark!"

"What? She can move and I'm a teacher."

The woman's perfectly primped hair was about to fall out from all the steam coming off the top of her head. Her blunt bob accentuates the harshness of her demeanor. Maybe that's why I didn't feel bad about taking him up on his offer. Everything in this place made me feel wholly inadequate. This was the same floor that saw designer shoes not dirty sneakers from the bargain bin. Even Mark had on some black patent leather shoes that were so clean I could see my reflection.

He nodded for her to hit play. "Follow me."

I allowed him to turn me around and guide me into a simple sway back and forth. As soon as the beat dropped he swung me away from him. I added my own little hair whip before he twirled me back into his embrace. Surprised that it had gone so well, we stared into each other's eyes. And I almost melted under his blue gaze. Then he led me into a two-step easily.

But what are my feet doing?

Why do I feel so nervous in his arms?

He smells so good.

This song plays in hell. Why is it so long?

I don't have two left feet. I have two right.

Why is he so damn cute?

This is kinda fun.

Thank God, it's over.

The thoughts in my head were playing fast and loose. And his idiotic smiling wasn't helping things. Why did he have to be hot?

"You actually did great."

I grinned madly. Until this moment, I didn't realize how much his opinion would matter to me. It was hard to even look him in the eye. I could feel the heat rising in my cheeks. And it was okay to accept the compliment because he didn't seem like the type to sugarcoat things. If he had said that I was horrible, then I would have ended up thanking dad for the career change. But as it stood I felt like Owen when he brings home a gold star on his homework.

"Who would have thought it? The tomboy can dance."

"Caliece——-"

She came and stood beside him, resting her hand on his shoulder. The very epitome of elegant beauty and I knew she always got the man she wanted. Life was handed to her on beds of pearls. Like a cat spraying, she was staking her claim. "Why are you even here?"

And suddenly, the place stunk. Her very presence made my stomach turn. I turned to Mark and tried to be as contrite as possible. "Would you believe that I came to apologize for the punch thing?"

He shook his head. "Try again."

"Would you believe that I mainly wanted to ask about Farmer's whereabouts?"

He shook his head from side to side. "That I believe. And I haven't seen him since he left for the fight."

"Thanks." I turned to leave, but stopped and turned back. "Did you get those items I signed? I am sorry."

He folded his arms across his chest. "I didn't want'em. But I did deserve that hit. So let me make it up to you. Let me turn you into a true dancer."

"Mark, I think your cockiness is misplaced here."

My mouth dropped open. I would have declined his offer if she had merely given me the chance. Instead, she was standing there insulting me. The fact that her nose wasn't broken was a testament to my new self-control.

"If you feel that way then let's bet on it."

"How so?" she asked, looking at me disdainfully.

"If I can't turn her into a dancer by D.D.C. Then I'll take your Saturday evening classes and you'll have more free time. If I win then you take my senior citizen classes over and I go a night without a pinched butt cheek."

I snickered at his last comment. My imagination ran wild at the thought of 80-year-old women chasing behind him in their walk-ers. But Michelle second to none Nunn wasn't no show poney. Okay maybe I was, but not to a bunch of stuck-up farts. Then I watched her turn positively red, resembling a spoiled teenager, mad that she got stuck with a pento instead of a Lamborghini and suddenly I badly needed to see her in that senior's class. "I'm in."

She huffed away, her heels clicking against the floor. Slamming the door behind her.

"After you punched me I did some cyberstalk-ing," he blurted out after a few moments, catching me off guard. "Your stats are pretty impressive. Why turn pro?"

I squelched a laugh because I was sure no one had ever asked me that. It's just automatically assumed that I'm in some war against the status quo. A middle finger to the world as a feminist. "Really it's just nice to be respected. Working so hard at any one thing leaves you craving recognition. I worked hard to get this far. I want to be the best at it and acknowledged for it."

"And now you're willing to try dance?"

"Most people would be *extra* offended, but I actually work better with my feet against the fire. It's going to be hard to make time for both, but I'm committed. I'd just like to keep this a secret if you don't mind."

He shrugged. "Fine by me."

"What, no questions?"

"No."

"Well, thank you." I looked back towards the door in no rush to leave. Feeling oddly content while talking about boxing of all things.

His confident voice knocked the cobwebs off my nether region. As I imagined him giving me a striptease that would rival Magic Mike.

"For what it's worth, you did make a believer out of me by the end of that fight. Before you hit me. I was just trying to save face with a friend."

"So boxing isn't just a male sport?"

Mark chuckled. "Listen, I never thought it was. I just hate to see a pretty face——-"

I cocked an eyebrow at him. A slightly wicked grin spread across his face as the rest of his words died on his tongue. Quickly, picking up that it was better to stay quiet.

"Watch your mouth," I teased, but not really. "This pretty face can rearrange yours."

I didn't know if I'd be able to put up with a man that didn't know that a woman's capabilities extended beyond the wedding ring and the pitter-patter of little feet. Even if he had me tingling all over. There was certainly a lot for me to think about it.

Chapter 7

That next morning, my thoughts were all over the place. Slightly annoyed that I didn't get to take the subway to work today because I could have used the time to stew over the conundrum I now found myself in.

"Are you really worried about this next fight?" Brooke asked as she locked her car, and we walked across the parking lot to the dance studio/gym.

I looked over at her curiously. Not sure what she meant. Had I said something out loud? My thoughts on everything that happened yesterday with Darren and Mark. Which was competing with the fight I had tonight. Thank God, that my workout today wouldn't be too strenuous. Keith just wanted me to work on my agility and movement. Having a good defense could be the difference between winning and losing. So I really couldn't take just one more thing on my plate. Instead, I waited for her to fill me in. Figuring that I'd missed some of the conversations on the ride over here.

"Michelle, you haven't said anything since I picked you up."

"Okay, this is big. So if I tell you, it has to come out of my mouth and sink right into the ground like it never existed."

Brooke gave me a curt nod. We always tried to work out together during the rare moments that Gideon allowed us to be in each other's orbit. We spend most of our nights talking each other's ears off about Gideon or the other guys in the gym. She was only five years older than me, but I considered her to be my big sister. I can trust her because she stayed hush on my relationship with Darren when she could sell us both out to some local tabloid.

"I caught Darren cheating again. The girl looked like she was barely old enough to drink." I hiked the bag higher on my shoulder, stopping just outside the studio.

"All I know is your next opponent better be wearing Darren's face. You'll never lose then."

Looking up at the sky, I exhaled loudly.

"It's not even cheating. Not really. It just feels that way because my last-ditch effort to turn this into something real left me crying in front of this place."

"Okay, sit," she replied, pulling me down to the sidewalk. "Why'd you end up crying here of all places?"

I placed my bag in front of me between my lap. "I don't know, I thought Farmer could cheer me up."

She screwed up her lip. "Yeah, but he doesn't know the truth about you and Darren, right?"

I looked up. "No, but we hold a mutual disliking for Darren that makes me feel better sometimes."

She came closer, lowering her voice so as not to be overheard. "I don't say this because I don't like to push you. But you know you can leave him if you're not happy, right? At some point, you have to stop choosing your career and choose yourself."

I gave her a reassuring smile. "Right."

"Even Queen Elizabeth had to decide to reign alone. And commit to that when everyone thought she was crazy."

I rolled my eyes. "Girl, get out of here."

I was about to tease her for even knowing who Queen Elizabeth was when the receptionist came barreling out the door.

"Oh, it's just you two? I thought I was going to have to shoo away some bums. Either way, you can't loiter here like that. It gives the place a bad name," she said waving her fingers down at us as if to show off her manicured nails or the huge rock on her finger. I couldn't be sure.

"We've both got to go change anyway."

I nodded and followed up behind her.

If I left Darren, how many people would I lose? My father? My management contract with Gideon? Sure, he respected my talent, but he sold ticket seats off of my relationship. I just pretended not to notice. Maybe the boxing community as a whole would abandon me? They were like an extended family of brothers and uncles all looking out for me. But men didn't have to worry about these kinds of what-ifs. Darren would just be applauded for his philandering. If he didn't out our arrangement out of spite.

A quick walk-through reception seemed to drain the color from some of the prospects' faces. It was easy to tell who wasn't used to seeing pure power walk by them. But I paid them no mind. As the receptionist led them on an impromptu tour of the place.

"This place is awesome. I can't believe that Farmer owns it. Have you heard anything?" she asked, heading into the changing room.

I groaned. "Just that this place was the original brainchild of his mother-in-law and his wife just recently took over. Or joined in or whatever. And some major ass-kissing had to be had for him to come back here."

The only thing Farmer's new sophisticated gym didn't have was changing rooms. That meant everyone had to share the rooms upstairs with the "fine china." A carefully crafted nickname for the dance teachers that was made up by a particularly sour boxer. During the two weeks this place had been open, I had no problem with it. However, there was a first for everything. Like dancing.

"When I came back in here I ran into Mark again. This time he asked if he could be my dance teacher. I said yes."

A silence fell over the room. Her dark eyes burrowed into mine in disbelief. "You did what?"

"I never should have told you," I said rolling my eyes. "He may be a jerk, but the idea isn't horrible."

Brooke did a weird inhale snort. "The cats out of the bag now. So you might as well let me save you from yourself."

"Am I committing suicide because I really don't think I need saving?"

I took one of the rooms next to hers. They weren't really rooms just white curtains that flowed floor to ceiling. I simply pushed them all the way around like hospital curtains. The velvet was thick enough to roll a body in. Or die from the dust. But the place was so immaculate that you couldn't do either. A matching white shaggy rug square under each room. One blue chair was shoved into each cubby. I sat down and discarded my shoes, one foot kicking off the other.

"Ain't you," Brooke quipped, pulling back her own curtain and disappearing. "Because I know you are not about to commit career suicide over some hot dance teacher."

"Pump your breaks. If I was going to do this it would be for me." My voice went down an octave. "I would finally have some fun."

"You know what's fun," she drawled, her steps muffled by the rug. "Winning. And you do that by staying focused."

She sounded like every guy I knew. Not that I was surprised. At least it was good practice if I ever had this conversation with any one of them. Taking a deep breath, I traded my jeans in for some sweats and a sports bra.

"Just give me time to figure out what I want to do," I asked, texting Shannon the details of my third fight tonight.

"Of course, but I'll be silently judging you. Meet you downstairs."

I smacked my lips, putting my gym shoes back on. After this, my phone was going on vibrate. It used to kill me knowing that I might miss a call from him. But those were the rules. Everyone wanted me focused and prepared to steamroll over the competition. I read her incoming text:

Auntie Shannon: So you want me to watch him tonight?

I erased what I was originally going to say and texted instead:

Michelle: No, bring Owen to the fight. Text dad for details.

Auntie Shannon: Fine, but you know how I feel about that.

She'd been nagging me about it since I started bringing him a year ago. But Owen deserves my full honesty. Even now he is old enough to understand but too young to see me get hurt. So I re-frame from bringing him often. But the more he was exposed to it the better. I wasn't turning into a doctor any time soon.

But when I left the changing room I found myself back in front of Studio One. Drawn to it like a beacon in the dark. Music and laughter drifted underneath the door of the class. Calling me through the closed door. Mark and Caliece were dancing together again.

I looked around for his friend and didn't see him.

But one thing was clear, Mark was talented. He came off as caring, but assertive in his instruction. I'd never been into dancers because I mistakenly believed them all to be gay. They certainly are a different breed of man. One that would appreciate the arts and would look down on the brutality of fighting. So I didn't break the barrier this time. No one goes to the garden to see the rocks. I would only be polluting the beauty of the moment.

He broke with his dance partner and our eyes connected as if my very thoughts drew him to me. A smile spread across his lips. Our eye contact made me nervous, but my father didn't raise no punk. A client came over and broke his gaze. "What are the odds that we would end up here together?"

"I was the one who gave Mark and Andrew the tickets. So I would say about 100%."

Farmer's voice caused me to jump. However, when I turned to face him a thought occurred to me. "You were the one that convinced him not to press charges."

"What? You expected the dirty car salesman Gideon to smooth things over," he murmured quietly in my ear, leading me away from the class.

"Or his equally as cool girlfriend, Caliece," I said jokingly. Hoping to reel in some information.

"Mark and Caliece aren't together, but it definitely was not her," he laughed.

He walked me down, and I almost tripped over my feet when I saw Darren in the middle of the ring. I was hoping that I wouldn't have to see him so soon. A bit out of sorts, I handed my bag to Farmer to put away. Trying to remind myself that to the outside world, Darren and I were happy.

"Ironclad out of the ring," Keith bellowed.

"Michelle needs to warm up with me," Darren said, dismissing his sparring partner.

I drew on three big gulps of air, trying not to hurl cuss words like gunshots at him. Instead, I managed a slick smile. "They don't need to see how we warm up."

I looked over to see my dad sitting on one of the leather couches. He wouldn't build me a pillow fort, but if Darren asked him to build a bridge across the Mississippi River, he'd ask for dimensions. I was almost positive that Darren's appearance today was dad's doing. We may have the same manager, but our workout schedules rarely over-lapped.

Making my way to the ring, Darren never took his eyes off me. Declaring to the crowd of onlookers, "I'd be open to a little voyeurism."

A few guys on the ground whistled as if they agreed.

"Woah," I said looking to Keith for help. "I've got a fight tonight. I don't need to be wearing myself thin."

"Battle of the sexes," someone in the crowd yelled.

Soon a mantra had started. "Do it. Do it."

"I'll do it. Shut up." Turning to Keith to get outfitted with sparring gloves.

I turned back to Darren, a shakiness in my limbs that I wish wasn't there. Any time Darren and I have sparred it's never gone well. "Is this a simple fight or something else? Just want to be ready. Then again you'd never be fair."

He made a jab at my face and I parried the punch. I could hear Keith yelling, "dance."

"Look at you still believing that life has to be fair," Darren whispered, throwing a few more punches at me.

"That's where you're wrong Darren. You and dad taught me that nothing in life is fair." Underestimating my check hook it landed harder than I intended. Hitting his jaw so hard that he staggered back.

"Round 1 over. Neutral corners."

Keith and Farmer were instantly in my ear giving me pointers. But as I turned back to Darren, there was a different look in his eyes. A clinch to his jaw indicated that he didn't take kindly to my little punch. The egotistical maniac now had something to prove to his bro buddies.

"Imaginary bell ring. Ding. Ding."

I groaned and rolled my eyes. Stepping out of the corner with my hands up. The only other boxing match I watched more than mine was his. I knew he would come back with the Jab. They wanted me to think on my feet so I combated that with some carefully maneuvered blocking.

However, a minute in I realized I had miscalculated. He had me trapped in the opposite corner. I was too busy defending my head and chest to fire any shots back.

I could hear Keith yelling, "Give him the slip."

But my arms were starting to physically burn from the force of me holding them up against the onslaught. He seemed to be getting cocky and reeled back to go in for the final blow. I used the reprieve to try to fire back, but I no longer had the force behind my jab. He countered by hitting me straight in my midsection. Knocking the wind out of me, and sending me hurtling towards the mat.

"Ay, Darren, back up. Leave her alone," Farmer shouted, hopping into the ring.

It felt like a 300-pound Gorilla was sitting on my chest. Inhaling hurt more than it should. I wanted to be the badass to stand up and shake it off. But I couldn't. "I think one of my ribs are broken."

Farmer helped me out of the ring and over to one of the empty couches next to my father. I leaned my head back and closed my eyes. Gritting my teeth as Farmer pressed certain spots on my chest that had me clenching the leather upholstery through my gloves.

"How bad is it?" My father asked.

"Just bruised. You're still cleared for tonight," Farmer confirmed. He wrapped his hand around my neck and forced me to look at him. "You're good."

I grit my teeth, looking over his head to my father. If I would never be more than just his money maker, the least he could do was protect his investment. And Darren wasn't rushing forward to apologize either.

I stood up quickly and pushed past them all. Landing another punch square in Darren's eye. "What the hell was that about? Maybe next time you'll see clearer before deciding to do some shit like that."

Farmer lifted me off the ground, physically pulling me away from him. "Cool out."

I shrugged away from his touch. "You tell him that. I got a fight tonight. That don't matter to nobody but me."

Gideon must've appeared out of nowhere like a mirage. "She's right. The whole thing is a money liability. This ain't gladiators. Keep the talent separate."

He returned to his office knowing that his word was bond. Farmer would certainly never overrule him. But I was out for blood. The lump of burning rage in my throat only seemed to be growing.

"What did I tell you about this unchecked temper of yours?" My dad whispered, his tone indicating a level of malice that was downright frightening.

Darren turned to my father with huge melancholy eyes. He was about to put on a show and I could only regard him with hard, angry eyes. "Maybe a lovers spat got the best of me. But I'd never intentionally ruin my baby's chances. Even if I had I'd still take care of you...two."

"No thanks."

The naked hostility in my dad's expression made me wonder if there wasn't more to Darren's words. Could dad be receiving money from me and Darren? Nah. I'd know if this oaf had extra cash. He had loose spending habits when it came to gambling and women. Darren was just making promises that he couldn't keep. It may not be the smartest decision, but if I needed to get rid of Darren I had to strike while the iron was hot. "Darren has like 5 rules that should never be broken on fight day. Yet what he just did was cardinal sin number one. Are you really telling me that's okay?"

"O-Okay, Michelle, laying it on a little thick aren't we," my dad teased, his gaze drifting between me and Darren. "Keith told you to split, but you weren't listening."

"Your bout starts in an hour and a half. We got to go," Farmer said interrupting.

I nodded following up behind him. The message was clear. Darren meant more to him than I ever would. Even when pitted against my own career.

Five rounds in, it was clear that I was losing this fight. All of Keith's and Farmer's advice was falling on deaf ears. However, this fight was also double my usual pay so losing wasn't an option.

"Anything about this fight familiar to you, Michelle?" Farmer asked as Keith applied ice to a swollen knot on the side of my face.

I could feel Gideon's hard gaze on me from the sidelines so I didn't answer. Everyone was disappointed and that was nothing new.

"Myra "Fusion" Moore's fighting style resembles Darren's fast and hard attack." He tapped the other side of my head to force me to look at him. "Maybe tonight's fight will end the same way this afternoon did, with your whining."

My leg shook furiously, the muted pain pounding in my head made it hard to feel anything, but anger.

"Stay out of the corner. If you find yourself boxed in, give her the slip. You can still win this if you fight smart."

Biting down on my bottom lip, I sucked in a harsh breath, as Keith applied an antiseptic to the cut on my nose. Once he was finished, I blurted to them both, "I've been fighting smart. Let's just face it, she's stronger than me."

Farmer's lips twitched downward. "Michelle, are you really thinking that you lost this? I can teach you every move ever invented. But I can't give you confidence."

He hurried out of the ring as the bell sounded. Every ounce of my being wanted to throw in the white towel. There is no plan once you're backed into a corner. The hits come in fast and furious like a bee sting. So maybe I did think I was going to lose, but that was only because I was.

And the final hit left me sprawling across the mat. My vision going in and out of focus. A vague sense of the referee counting. The people in my corner screaming. Darkness threatened to consume me like a comfy blanket.

"Mom, it's me, Owen." I hear my son yell from the edge of the ring. Crawling to the source of the sound I managed to make it to my knees.

"I used to be so mad at you for fighting." Tears streamed down his face as he choked back his sobs. "But I'm not anymore. You can beat her if you try. Grandpa said in high school, you were a superhero for a stupid girl. Be my superhero. I promise I'm not mad anymore. Just kick butt."

I made it to my feet on the ninth count, whispering, "I love you."

"Are you okay to continue?" The referee asked, holding my wrists.

"Just move out the way," I snapped back.

The bell rang, signaling the end of round five. I muttered "fuck" under my breath knowing I only had two more rounds to pull through.

"What did little man say to you?" Farmer shouted.

"Something I needed to hear. Now tell me how to win this. I'm listening." This was a new fight. I attacked the seventh round with a fervor that came from the very bowels of my belly.

In the eighth round, I landed a bolo punch that sent Myra down for the count. We were finally on equal footing. I felt better about my stance at the ring of the bell.

"You really pulled this through kid," Farmer spouted, handing me a bottle of water.

The announcer appeared in the middle of the ring. "By split decision, still reigning undisputed featherweight champion, Michelle 'second to none' Nunn."

He raised my hand high in the air. I yanked away from him to lift Owen into my arms. Darren stayed outside the ring, blowing kisses. While my dad waved. I ignored them both pretending that the crowd blocked my view.

An arm snaked around my waist, and I looked over to see Gideon pulling me in for a professional photo with a photographer. "If you give up like that again. I'm dropping you. That's the only game Gideon doesn't play."

Relinquishing his hold on me, I looked up at Owen who hadn't heard a thing. Letting him down from my shoulder. I cut my eyes at Gideon. "Yes, sir."

"Congratulations, princess peach," My auntie smiled, coming up to give me a hug. My vision blurred from unshed tears. My physical pain was nothing to my emotional wounds.

Chapter 8

It had only been a week or so, but Ever Fit could star on one of those before and after home makeover shows. They went from having no gym equipment to four heavy bags and two free-standing quick punchers. Some heavy-duty rope hung on the wall outside the ring. But it was the modern touches that gave this place a more professional feel. The black leather lounge couches, and the free-standing counter for a receptionist. Gideon's sparse gym had me thinking that I should probably thank Farmer's ex-wife for this. But I could hardly enjoy the makeover thanks to Farmer and Gideon's screaming over last night's fight.

They dismissed me once they realized that I was numb to it all. So it wouldn't be the last time that I'd be hearing about my controversial win. To them, the win doesn't matter if it's marred by my indecision. I was just glad dad hadn't shown up for this heart-to-heart.

But when I got upstairs the receptionist's computer was tuned to the news and my son's face was sprawled across it.

"Oh, I'm sorry," she said, clicking away from the screen.

"No, I need to see that." I came up behind the younger woman, my eyes stuck on the screen.

She seemed hesitant but went back to the other screen. The end of the video showed me lifting Owen into my arms. "The video of this little boy giving his mother a pep talk during the fight was taken by our local KBBM news station."

The camera panned to the newscaster's partner. "It's almost hard to marry this woman to the same one that knocked out the fan."

"Yeah, this definitely humanizes her. I'm even realizing just how hard it is to be a female, a mother, and still be able to achieve your dreams in a male-dominated occupation. So good luck to her."

I looked up from the screen as Farmer and Gideon appeared. Both appeared as if they needed to shed their skin like snakes after our meeting together. There was still the matter of contracts. "Hey, Gideon. 30%."

He pounded his fist in the air.

"It's about time that we start to make some real money," Farmer grinned, clapping Gideon on the back. Leaving much happier than they were before.

"Thanks again," I said, to the woman. Upon a closer look, she couldn't be any older than sixteen. This was my first time seeing her around. The original receptionist must be out sick. So I found myself swearing her to secrecy as well. It was better if everyone thought I left for the day. Gideon and Farmer were gone, but the gym was still open until late.

I looked towards the door hesitantly, but fear kept me from going in. My newfound fame was telling me not to bother. Dancing was a kid's dream and I was a grown woman fighting for some serious cheddar. My dad would want me to focus on that.

He always made it clear that boxing wasn't just a career it was a lifestyle. It was how I was going to feed myself and Owen because he didn't give birth to no Einstein. And I wasn't a princess.

Adding to my confusion were Mark's comments that I was actually pretty good at this dancing thing. It certainly helped that I thought I saw something close to desire, shrouding his face when we danced. I stood up straight and knocked confidently on the door before entering.

A wide grin spread across his face. "You're here."

"Mark, we're practicing. You don't have time to entertain boxers." Making it known that she disapproved.

He released his hold on Caliece and marched towards me. Holding out his hand as if I belonged there. "Yeah, but we're done."

My heart did a little dance at his emphasis on the word *done*. Just happy to know that he didn't feel like my whole existence as a boxer was beneath him. Not that he was completely on my side either. I still remembered his comment from the other day. Briefly wondered if I blended into the floor with the way they were still talking as if I weren't there. They proved once again that power wasn't always in how much one could bench press. My lips pursed, they may not be lovers, but they argued like siblings.

It was little wonder that Mark thought all women were helpless damsels with pretty smiles. Caliece didn't look like she could open a jar of pickles by herself. Was that what he found sexy? Riding in on a white horse to save his woman from fermented cucumbers. In another universe, I could totally picture him riding on the back of a noble steed. The muscles in his arms dripped with sweat after taming a wild horse.

I inhaled audibly, wishing more than anything that Caliece wasn't here at all. Briefly, her deep green eyes met mine with a smirk. We were as opposite as night and day. My athleticism derived from my boxing career, and I had none of the gentleness and agility that dancers needed. My toned arms lifted weights and there was no grace in its form like Caliece. I just seemed wrong in comparison.

But I wasn't jealous. I was used to male attention completely underestimating me and looking me over for the pretty blond next to me. It was just hard not to compare myself to this classic beauty. She was perfectly wrapped like a Christmas present too extravagant for cheap wallets. And I was faux crocodile leather. To break the tension, I said, "What was that song?"

"Shoulder of Orion by Lazerhawk."

Looking very thin-lipped as she came to stand beside Mark. Her very stance of that of a boutique store mannequin. She'd never slouch over a beer with the guys.

"I think I've heard of them."

"Of course you have."

"This is actually Caliece's first go-round with this type of music. We're trying different songs out for the Discover Dance Championship," Mark filled in for me.

"Yes, I'm more at home among classical fair."

"Of course you are," I replied, mimicking her condescending tone.

"I just hope that your love for music translates into dance. If not you can always go back to what you do best, hitting people."

He wagged a finger at her. "I'm going to have to respectfully disagree."

Caliece walked towards the door. "Once glass is broken. Even when it's put back together it never looks the same way."

My mouth dropped open. And the only comfort I had was my father's voice in my head saying never let them see you cry.

"Ignore her," he said, going over to the radio.

I plastered on a smile. "So teach, what do I call you?"

"Mark. Wade. Mr. Wade. It's up to you and your comfort level."

"We could probably just keep it Mark. And Michelle is fine for me too. None of that second-to-none crap here."

His face was somewhat obscured in the mirror by the baseball cap on his head. The words Chicago, sprawled across it in white. I tried not to admire his lean frame, but it was hard not to notice the rippling muscles through the arm of his shirt. Now, it kinda angered me that a woman like Caliece might actually be his type.

And it was stupid that it angered me. This was just about dancing and nothing else. Obviously, I was only noticing these things because he was my type. Mark was smaller than Darren, but not by much. Darren was a heavyweight when Mark would measure in as light heavyweight. An inch shorter than the man, both their bodies were defined and muscular. The only major difference was Darren's blond hair fell to his shoulder's and Mark seemed to keep his jet black hair short with messy spiky hair and a low tapered fade. It wasn't until I had taken off my shoes and put on fresh socks that I realized that he hadn't looked at me since Caliece left.

I sighed heavily feeling condemned. Friendly bedfellows next to guilt and shame. But now I was also insecure and had never felt so ugly; manly and gross. Swallowing down my sorrow, I decided to face his arrogance head-on.

Dammit.

I frowned and exhaled loudly. "I'm a fighter."

The first few times he had seen me, I was completely healed from my fights. Now, looking in the mirror I could scare a clown. Maybe he hadn't realized until now just what he had gotten himself into. At least I knew what he had in common with Caliece. They were both surface-level deep, and he couldn't be any older than 33 or 34. Little boys never grow up.

"Did you hear me? I'm a fighter. It ain't always going to be pretty. If you think this is bad, you should see the other girl. This is my career. I thought you at least respected that, but if you're somehow uncomfortable with it all then I'm ready to bounce."

He exhaled and finally looked up. Marching across the floor to stand in front of me. His gaze assessed me from top to bottom. "Turn your head left then right."

I should deck him. Instead, I gave him the benefit of the doubt and did as I was told. Feeling self-conscious about the huge knot on the side of my left eye. Or the black marks underneath them.

"Did that hurt?"

"No." Just my pride.

He placed his hands on either side of my back. "Put your arms on top of mine."

I sighed, this was getting old. Was this how he taught? Or was I merely being sized up by a Caliece-sized measuring tape?

"Anything hurt or ache? A pulling sensation."

"Nope." I had a cut-man and his name was Keith. What did any of this have to do with him being an asshole? If I was too ugly to work with at least be man enough to say so.

He wrapped his arms around my waist and lifted me a few feet off the ground. Holding me firm against him. My breath caught in my throat, as my heart was sent spinning. He even cradled my thigh against his hip. Sending my flower screaming for him to touch every petal. "How about now?"

My body was certainly confused. "No," I croaked.

He put me down and stepped back. Leaving me reluctantly craving his touch. "I was hesitating because I wasn't sure how to approach this. But since we're being real. I wont be changing my teaching style because you are a boxer."

I frowned. Who asked him too?

"Out there it's par for the course for you to get hurt and no one blinks an eye. It's just fine. But in here my main concern is you. Dancing requires a different type of fortitude. You've got to be mentally and physically sound."

I stood up a little straighter. "I accept that."

"That means if you can't follow my instructions, I throw in the white towel. If you get hurt before or during dancing, I throw in the white towel. If beating somebody's ass got you so tired that you can't remember left from right, I throw—"

"I throw in the white towel. I get it, Sir. Wade." Standing at attention.

He looked at me grimly. "There's no push through anyway. The show must go on. Pain is not a weakness. There's just you and your comfort. And you've got to trust me by telling me the truth."

I nodded.

He touched my forehead lightly. "Now, how's your head? No headaches."

"No."

"You'd tell me if it was?" He asked. His touch made it hard to think. This was definitely more than an examination, it was practically a caress. Maybe he liked me more than he was ready to let on. Well, this chauvinist could keep dreaming.

"Yes, grandpa," I laughed.

"Okay, let's take today easy then young whippersnapper. Just show me what you can do. Will use the song, Shoulder of Orion, from earlier."

Feeling a bit nervous, I closed my eyes and tried to get a feel of the music naturally. It had a building beat with a forward momentum that was almost better for the beginner in me than the first song. I felt sexy, dangerous. And almost sensing that he fed my energy. None of our steps were recognizable. At least not to me. Our movements were fluid and unrestricted by rules. In fact, it almost felt like we were in a club of our own making.

It wasn't until his hands had left my waist to caress my face that I found it hard to breathe. My body was receptive to his every touch. I wasn't silly enough to think he was going to kiss me. But tell that to my body. It certainly wasn't professional to be reacting this way.

So as soon as the song reached a quiet point, I pulled away. My mind kept wandering back to his words. Was I getting too used to brushing my pain underneath the rug? I had never given it much thought. But that was kind of telling on its own. At home, mommy had to be positive 100% of the time and have no pain. Coming to work with the pain, just meant I had to push through it. And I purposely hid any slight tingle from Farmer so as not to appear weak. My only option was to compartmentalize and pretend like it was all nothing.

"Hey, since this is your first time we can stop early."

"That would be good," I said, suddenly feeling tired.

"Let's meet again Tuesday evening."

I nodded. His patience and understanding during practice should make me happy, but instead, I was just mad. It was like he was making me like him.

Chapter 9

During the short week, I've spent with Mark he's always made it his business to consider my feelings. He doesn't make me choose between dancing and boxing and works with my demanding schedule. If the roles were reversed I wouldn't get the same courtesy from Farmer or Gideon. But they also don't make me laugh like Mark.

Most of the time he just taught me a step and watched me practice it over and over alone. He only jumped in once he felt like I had it down. During our last class, he let me hear the song he picked for our win. Which made me even more excited for today's class.

There's something about us dancing together that made me feel like Ginger Rogers. I might actually be capable of singing in the rain. My body also preferred when we danced close together. His arms around me like a Snuggie. This kind of happiness felt good. Even when it felt like I was running a marathon on both ends.

"We've got to work on your continuous movement. No rest stops. Follow through. Let's dance together."

I nodded, wiping the sweat from my brow. His critique reminded me that he was just my teacher. Steering my thoughts back to my dance technique.

"Don't worry about being off beat."

I walked toward him slowly, and his eyes seemed to measure my every step. After he took the position, I found it hard to tear my eyes away from him to look to the left as the dance required. As easy as it was to work with him, it could also be intimidating. Sometimes it felt like the heat from his eyes warmed my skin, but it could be the dance.

Especially when it turned me into an awkward nerd every time he touched me. I'm looking at his thick defined fingers that might one day skip across my belly. He opened a flat palm, and I curled my hand around his. Seconds later, he clasped my hand in his and it offered up its own security. With that one hand, he could take me anywhere if I merely trusted him.

Thinking these types of thoughts about my dance teacher wasn't the best thing either. When he entered my dance space it was hard for me to breathe, and focus on the steps. Truthfully, as much as I wanted a father/daughter dance or a moonlight dinner slow dance under the stars. I was happy that Mark was my first dance partner.

He spun me away from him and I twirled like a ballerina. Returning effortlessly to hold without the crash landing of her first encounter. I know that I was supposed to be working on my continuity, but I had to pause. My hand lingering in his.

"Yeah, you just did that."

My eyes welled up with tears. I'm instantly overwhelmed by this simple, but momentous occasion. I'm almost unrecognizable. I actually felt beautiful.

"Hey, what's going on there?" he asked gently, wiping at a rogue tear with his index finger.

"I did it."

"And you're capable of doing a whole lot more. Just let me teach you."

"Okay," I choked out.

"If I teach this mockingbird to dance will you stop all the tears?"

"Shut up." I laughed and punched him on the arm. This boy was awful cute. Suddenly, the rational part of my brain kicked into overdrive and told me to step away from the misogynistic beefcake. The hormones from my crying just had me feeling all wonky. It's bad enough that he doesn't view women as capable of being able to take care of themselves. I didn't need to prove that I couldn't avoid his charms either.

He nodded slightly for us to begin again. I grabbed his hand and put the other on his shoulder. But he looked thoughtful, "Let's change the music. It's a little distracting and it's early. We just need something fun to set the mood."

"Just out of curiosity, why do you close your eyes when you dance? You don't do it a lot. I just noticed."

"Dancing blind is the ultimate sign of trust. Plus I feel like I predict your movements better when I'm not wholly reliant on sight."

He hurried back to my side as if I were a skittish bird that might fly away and disappear. But I've never been that delicate. Which caused me to chuckle a bit. This cute fantasy just became a small crush. Before I put on the serious face that the dance needed.

Television Romance by Pale Waves began to play.

He squeezed my hand as a signal cue. It was the first time, I understood why colonials used to think that hand-holding might lead to debauchery. Right now, I wanted to take that hand and guide it all over my body.

What would that be like? Would he instantly set off small forest fires that would only be put out by the use of his tongue? Kneading the dough of my thighs until they felt like butter in his hands. Or would he tangle his fingers in my ponytail and give it a tug to show me who's boss.

Somewhere, my thoughts become reality.

Our dance didn't resemble anything we were doing earlier. It felt like we were dancing underneath the stars. The crystal chandeliers were no more than little sparks of fire. My head had a mind of its own as it came to rest on his shoulder. His chin resting on top of my head. Our chests pressed together. It felt so natural. As if we both needed this moment together. I looked up into his eyes and they seemed to shine with need. My body was very aware that neither one of us had yet to step out of reach. The corners of his mouth turned down hinting at his regret. Demanding answers to questions that I didn't even know.

It was beautiful.

Too beautiful.

I couldn't mentally sustain anything this good.

He dipped me over his arm. "Trust me. More fluidity as you lean over. I'll never drop you."

My mind focused on him like some sort of homing beacon. The hard line of his jaw beckoned me to trace its contours. I couldn't help but imagine how those same taut muscles would respond to my kiss. I inhaled sharply through my nose and exhaled through my mouth as he stood me back on solid ground. My senses were firing on all cylinders as his hand moved from my waist to trail along my jawline. His touch alone left me salivating at the mouth. Like a huge sundae had been placed before me. My squelched lust demanded to know which flavor he tasted like. Positive that my heart sounded like a race car by now.

He's staring at me now and we've completely stopped dancing. I can practically see the questions turning in his mind like Rolley Polley. He's not sure if he should kiss me. That would make two of us. In my fantasies, this decision is a lot easier. But in reality my obligations reign supreme.

"I never asked you how you felt after the fight?"

"I'm okay, battling at about 75%. It could be worse."

His eyes dropped to my lips. "If I forget to ask you that again, feel free to clip me on the back of the head."

I smiled. "Did you just give me permission to hit you again, because you know I will?"

"I'm sure, I can take it." He slid his hand around my neck. His head hovering just above mine.

Was the music loud enough to drown out my chaotic breathing? It had to be because it was also making it hard to think. Maybe I just wanted to know what his kiss felt like. Normally, I'm not this nervous in the sex department on flirtation lane. Had it always felt this heart-stopping being with him?

Instinctively I tilted my head towards him. My hand pressed against his chest. It revealed that he wasn't the only one on a roller coaster ride right now. His heartbeat was strong and insistent. Darren preferred I not touch him at all. While Owen's father had preferred for me to be the aggressor. Yet with Mark, I found myself following his lead. Right off of Niagara Falls into a crystal clear pool of passion and want. He only needed to seal the deal.

"Hey, Mark I wanted to ask you———. How much time are you devoting to teaching her?"

Caliece's voice breaks through the atmosphere like a shrill drill. Severing our connection as if it were a red bow and she was the scissors. Mark dropped his hand and stepped back. For a moment we just stared at each other. But when I looked at him I saw Mark. But who does he see when he looks at me? Darren, Caliece, or someone like her. The desire in his eyes gave way to confusion before settling on regret. I watched him mirror my feelings. The only thing that was missing was, hurt. My emotions were a flurry of punches aimed straight at my head.

"We don't have time for that."

I rolled my eyes. She must not have seen anything because there was no way that she would lead with that. Of course, it was too much to hope that she would just stick to the subject of dance without the added drama. Then again I was crushing on someone she obviously wanted. Was I giving off some sort of thirsty pheromone that she could sniff out?

"It's my free time and it doesn't exactly affect us does it?" he said, running his hands over the scruff on his face.

"Of course it does. You'll be more rundown and unfocused the longer this continues."

"I know how to be careful Caliece. I do have full-time classes in addition to the competition with you."

My gaze darted between the pair, and I started to get annoyed. They were talking about me as if I wasn't here, again. I crossed my arms in front of my face. Trying to ignore the fact that all I wanted to do was dance with him again. Be in his arms.

Should I quit now?

Our almost kiss was spontaneous. It could be a rare occurrence like pulling off a corkscrew punch. We weren't in an all-out affair.

"I mean granted, Miss Nunn would never understand, but you should know better."

I laughed. This was all a little comical. She had to see our almost kiss because she couldn't be this dramatic over just dancing. "It's true that I don't have any prior dance experience. But Mark is extremely capable. If he couldn't handle our schedule, he would tell me."

"Maybe, but he's not really doing anything profound here either. It's a meaningless distraction. Whatever you learn will be beaten out of you later."

"Don't go there, I always make sure she's in dancing shape."

There he was speaking for me again. Well, not this time. "You can speak for her, but not me. Caliece just needs to watch what she says about me."

She laughed. "Or what you're going to hit me too?"

"Okay girls, let's calm down."

Ignoring him I said, "Are you kidding? I'm not going to bruise my hand on that face of stone. Tell me what's your heart made of, Golden Wood Granite, from the Italian shores of Spain."

"Do what you want with this loser. Will talk later." She stormed out without a backward glance.

Yet, I felt like I was the one who had lost. My heart was telling me to pick up where we had left off. But my head knew that it was time for me to quit. My head wanted to go home and rest on my aunt's shoulder with a bag of unhealthy chips and soak the scars forming on my heart. "I'm sorry If I disrespected your partner."

I've been waiting for someone to tell her off for the longest. Caliece is a great dancer, but she's annoying. Our relationship is strictly professional and we're kind of stuck with each other."

"Do you think the bet is still on?"

"Oh, I'm almost certain it is. Caliece is going to be rooting for your demise."

My eyebrows went up a notch, but I wasn't concerned.

"We should call it a night," he volunteered. Putting distance between us as he went back to the radio. "So I'll see you on Thursday."

"Right," I said, taking the reprieve.

I walked over to the shelving case and grabbed my bag and shoes. Finding it more comfortable to dance in my socks than in gym shoes. But I hated moist, funky socks. So I had to change them and now I was going through 2 or 3 pairs a day. And whipping out my feet after a sexy moment is the ultimate embarrassment. I was definitely not one of Mark's beauty queens. After this, he shouldn't be interested in me.

Not at all sad that the sexy moment was lost. We were obviously attracted to each other. And from his response, we shared the same ambivalent feelings. I wanted to avoid falling for a talented chauvinist. He probably hated that I wasn't his type. Which should be insulting, but it's not. He's not mine either. Going from Darren to Darren lite was not a good choice. At least Darren knew how important boxing was.

I just grabbed my things as quickly as I could. The memory of the kiss was in the forefront of my mind. Anything between us would be a losing fight.

Never go into a fight expecting to lose.

Chapter 10

Our almost kiss was all I could think about for the past two weeks. It would have been everything I dreamed about. Then again it was only a product of the atmosphere, music, and chandelier stars. That was enough to explain why I romanticized being with him. So there was no need for my stomach to be tied up in a messy bow over him.

Which is why I made up excuses to miss practice. Instead, I was working out longer at the gym. Under the guise, that fight four called for my full attention. Now that it was here, I was starting to think that I should quit dancing altogether. It wasn't fair to simply push things back with poor explanations. But I didn't think I could handle being in the same room with him again without jumping his bones.

The feeling of his lips brushing my cheek was a constant reminder of everything I couldn't have. A life that at one time I desperately wanted. But he was still doing that macho thing. I don't need anyone speaking for me. Losing one's voice is the first freedom to go in oppression. Then one day your left wondering when you stopped being a whole person. The sum of who I am was whatever Darren or my father said about me. I was young before, but now I'd never allow someone to take my voice again. I'd rather die alone and never marry. Then risk being unseen in another relationship.

"You're distracted, Michelle, should I be worried?" Farmer asked, his aggravated voice cutting through the music coming in on my headphones. He was holding the door open and I had no idea for how long.

My attitude immediately shifted. "She's dead."

Living up to that statement was harder than I thought. My focus was split and I wasn't fighting like I usually do. It was all happening so fast and it was like I was moving in a blur. Twenty minutes later I'm in my fourth fight, sixth round, and my opponent was clearly lifting her feet with every punch. A few well-timed combos would knock this girl clean off her feet. Leaving her with a penalty in my favor. Yet, I had yet to complete the payoff because all I could think about was him.

The bell rang and we both went to our neutral corners. I spit out my mouth guard in to Keith's hand. Meanwhile, the look Farmer gave me was pleading, giving me a drink of water.

"This fight can be over. You know what to do."

I spit out the water into a bucket before Keith put my mouthguard back in. Ignoring his words because I already know what they will be. Instead, my gaze fluttered over the crowd. My preemptive 30% was right on track. For the first time, since I started this I was finally going to see some success. Maybe even make enough to prepay my rent.

"You hear me?" Farmer backed.

I refocused on my enemy sitting across the ring. "I got it."

Banging my gloves together and coming out of the corner on the bell with my gloves swinging. Farmer was right, it was time to get down to business. This was for the rent money. It wasn't until they were announcing that I was the winner that I even realized that the fight was over. Or the fact that Farmer held me around my waist to keep me from going after the girl again. It felt like I had blacked out and emerged into a different world. The crowd mixed as they cheered and jeered my behavior.

Back in the changing room with Gideon and the rest of my team, I was still fired up. I yelled to whoever was closest to take off my gloves. Once off, Gideon placed the $50,000 check in my hand and I was positively shaking. I'd never held so much money before. This was still for the rent, but I'd actually have enough left over to throw my dad an, *I love you fee*. And still, have money put away for Owen's college fund.

It was at that moment that I laid down the law. I would ride this wave until it collapsed. No more fights for less than 30%. Gideon added his own stipulations. I ended up agreeing to release a small clip promoting the new gym location before having Owen interrupt me with some good luck wishes. This video will be released 30 minutes before my next fight. It felt like everything that I had poured into boxing including my heartache it was finally paying me back.

There was no way that I could quit now.

I even stayed later after everyone had left. Stepping in the middle of the ring, this time fully dressed. Trying to imagine myself with the belt around my waist, determined steel in my eyes. And a loser wishing she was me. It did feel good.

"Can I take you home?"

I shielded my eyes against the lone light that had been left on to see Mark standing just outside the ring. The train was usually a brutal ride home if I ended up being too tired. And I could already feel the exhaustion creeping into my muscles. No more running. "Okay."

I leaned down between the ropes. My bag slid off my shoulder and got a little tangled. I yanked hard feeling a little weird that he was even here.

He rushed over and helped me with my bag. Throwing the duffel over his shoulder. "Good fight today, it was like you went feral on that chick. It was cool to watch."

"It wasn't my best fight, but I pulled it out."

We were silent for most of the ride over. Me, replaying the, I quit script, in my head a hundred different ways. None of which reached my lips. I needed that time to unscramble my heart and decide what I want for Owen and me.

A clearer head had slowly been revealing itself over the past couple of weeks. And tonight just confirmed what I was thinking. I was finally at the cusp of something great, and I couldn't simply back away. My feelings for him were already more than they should be. I cleared my throat, "I think—"

"We let the song and dance take over." He finished for me.

Seconds later, the car hit a pothole that caused him to swerve before he righted it again. He cursed but thanked God that there were no cars coming in the opposite direction. I simply stared at the slowly passing street lights. I knew that we wouldn't pass a single one until we made our way back to my neck of the woods. The brief scare allowed us to retreat into our thoughts.

He was definitely on to something. I had wondered the same thing. They weren't really our feelings. Those feelings belonged to the dance. I should have considered that before. "At least now we don't have to set another date to practice."

"Don't quit."

My gaze flew from the passing scenery to his eyes. I chewed on my bottom lip. "Tonight was my best payday since I started."

His shoulders slumped and he looked defeated.

"Look we don't have to talk about this."

A few seconds pass and my phone vibrated. I pulled it out and read a text by my aunt:

Auntie Shannon: Are you almost home?

I quickly replied back:

Michelle: Yes, getting a ride from my dance teacher.

Auntie Shannon: Ohhh, I want to meet him.

Michelle: Fat chance.

I sent the text quickly and put my phone on silent before she could send anything else. Tucking the phone back into the duffel that sat at my feet.

He sighed. "We don't have to talk about this, but I want you to know that I get it."

My upper lip curled in disdain. "Get what exactly? That I've finally found something outside of boxing and I have to leave it. The only reason I could do it as long as I did was because I'm hiding one part of my life from the other. And dancing means that we have to be close, too close."

"You have a boyfriend. I'm not going to forget that ever again. You're in these classes to learn to dance. Caliece coming in was just perfect because it stopped us from getting carried away."

"We've been dancing together for a little while now. Your friend would consider you a traitor. And Darren would have my head."

"Okay, but friends don't always have to agree. But your guy should support you in having fun."

"He supports me winning my bouts. Not the tap-dancing pulling me away from practice."

He looked over at me before switching lanes. "Didn't know you were the type to let a man dictate what she can and can't do. You hit a man in the nose because he disrespected your career. Our almost kiss was all I could think about for the past two weeks. It would have been everything I dreamed about. Then again it was only a product of the atmosphere, music, and chandelier stars. That was enough to explain why I romanticized being with him. So there was no need for my stomach to be tied up in a messy bow over him.

"Just remember, your boyfriend shouldn't get a say in how you spend your time."

I stretched the seat belt over my chest. Feeling like I had to stick up for myself. "I know all we do is dance, but what about the way that we danced today. Do you think any man would have cheered that on? No. The next person punched would have been you, but not by me."

I was a coward, but Mark wasn't allowed to know that. Plus, there was much more at play here than hurt feelings. Although his poor opinion of me was setting off some pained nerves and I just wished that his opinion didn't matter.

"I'm sorry if I complicated things for you."

"Yeah, so you've said."

"Michelle, if dance ignited a new fire inside you. You can't simply snuff it out by refocusing on something else. It will eat you alive until you're hollow inside. And the only thing that feels good is your feet on that dance floor. Even if you don't dance with me. You're going to regret quitting."

"I already regret it."

Mark looked over at me, curiosity in his expression. "I think we made it."

I kept my gaze low and opened the car door.

Chapter 11

"Woohoo, up here!"

I knew that voice anywhere.

"Hey, dance teacher."

He unbuckled his seat belt and leaned over the steering wheel to peer through the windshield. A grin on his face, he said, "I think she's talking to us."

"Yeah, it's my aunt." Half her body was leaning out the window. Her low-cut top, revealed a healthy portion of cleavage. Unable to even look at Mark I covered my eyes with my hands. I guess I was never too old to be embarrassed by my relatives. When I looked up again there was no hiding the displeasure on my face.

Mark was already halfway out of the car, squinting up at the night sky. "Yes, ma'am?"

The ceiling lamp illuminated her like she was some angel in disguise. What if Mark's type was older women? I had been rooting for my aunt to find someone for the longest. But not my maybe dance-infused crush.

"Come upstairs, let me meet you." She disappeared back inside as if her word was the only thing needed. He was instantly entranced and had to follow. I almost wanted to laugh. How does one go about having that type of confidence? It certainly wasn't hereditary. I was sorely lacking in the sexual wilds category. I shut the passenger side door. "Well, you heard the woman. Come on up."

"That's really sweet of you to invite me," he grinned, as he fell into step beside me.

Tongue in cheek, I cut my eyes at him. "Don't get cocky, I still haven't made up my mind whether to quit or not."

Mark jogged ahead and opened the door for me. He dramatically waved me in and I'm already starting to regret my aunt's window outburst. We climbed the three flights of steps to the top without saying a word. But as we made it to my floor, he touched my elbow to stop me.

"I know it's not fair for me to spout off about your relationship. But can you at least tell me I'm wrong?"

"About what?"

"You need to start taking care of yourself first. Before you worry about other's opinions."

I rolled my eyes and turned back to my door. A door that opened as soon as I turned the knob. Way to keep it cool auntie."

"Nice to finally meet you, young man."

"You as well," he said, coming up to kiss her graciously on the cheek. "I'm Mark."

"I just wanted to meet the man that got this woman back on her toes. She hasn't mentioned dancing since I use to sneak her tiara's as a kid."

My smile faded slightly at the mention of her sneaking me girly toys.

"It happened by accident," Mark replied. If he found something wrong with my aunties last statement, he didn't let on."

My aunt led him further into the living room. Indicating that she intended for this video to be more than just a simple stop-through. I fell in line and sat next to him on the couch. Making sure to keep my distance. His touch affected me in ways I don't want to think about.

Owen hadn't appeared from his room and for that I was grateful. I wasn't opposed to him meeting the people in my life. But I was conscious of the fact that Mark was still a big secret. And a child shouldn't be plunged into an adult's business.

"Hopefully, now that she has gotten a taste, I can convince her to keep going with her lessons."

"So are you single, Mark?"

"Auntie," I pleaded, through gritted teeth.

He turned to me and smirked, but all I could manage to do was avert my eyes. "Yes, I'm single."

"Single huh." Nodding her head as if that was the most interesting news since, Al Capone's vault. I tried to plead with my eyes for her to stop. Besides, I already knew that. If she was going to be helpful she should find out what his type was. "Now why would a handsome guy like you still be single with no children or ex-wives?"

"Yeah, no children. Or wives, ex or otherwise," he clarified.

My eyes darted to the hallway as Owen appeared marching angrily into the bathroom. Not bothering to even glance into the living room. That was definitely not like my curious boy.

"Listen…"

"Shannon. Aunt Shannon."

He smiled. "Aunt Shannon, Michelle, and I see a lot of each other at night after she works out and on the weekends. I get to see how stoic she is. Yet, unintentionally funny in a sarcastic way. I always saw her as beautiful." Looking back at me, he wet his lips. "She's dangerous and super talented. And capable of more than even she realizes. But I'm not in the business of stealing love. My girl is going to belong to me and no one else. Michelle is already spoken for and he's super lucky."

His smile ended up drawing one out of me.

Auntie Shannon nodded as if she approved of his answer. "If she replaced him, no one in this house would miss him."

I caught another glimpse of Owen stomping back to his room and slamming the door. Drawing my attention away from my aunt and her poor matchmaking. "Excuse me a sec."

"So how did you get into dance?" My aunt asked.

I didn't need to hear the answer. My thoughts were already focused on my son. And all I wanted to do was fight the something or someone that changed his mood so drastically. I opened the door cautiously. "Owen, it's mommy."

"Go away," he whined. His head hanging off the bed as he played on his portable GameBoy. "I don't want to talk to you or Auntie Shannon."

"Can I ask you what you're not talking to us about?" I questioned. "Everything seemed okay yesterday at pick up. Are you angry that I got home late today?"

"No. Why would my mom beating up people instead of being at home make me angry?"

And there it was. It was my fault. He didn't even look up when I came in. I try to be a time warrior in order to avoid situations like this, but today I failed.

"Look at me, sweetie." I came and sat on the bed beside him. "You know without asking that you're the most important thing to me.

And if I made you feel otherwise then that's for me to fix. So tell me what you need." Trying unsuccessfully to catch his defiant gaze.

"Just quit!" He screamed, rolling away from me. In doing so it revealed a small reddish welt across his upper forearm. The gray sleeve of worn batman shirt riding up. How could I have missed it? He had gotten into some long sleeve pj's early yesterday. I remember thinking it was weird.

"Owen, what happened to you?" I asked, touching the rope-like welt gently.

"Nothing," he said jerking away from me.

He seemed determined to put me on mute and wasn't volunteering anything else. So I grabbed his wrist and half dragged him out the door to the living room. Where Auntie Shannon was still entertaining Mark. He was the furthest thing from my mind now that mommy mode had switched on. They both quieted as I approached. "What happened?"

Auntie Shannon gulped and cleared her throat awkwardly. "You were so tired yesterday that there wasn't much time to talk. The school let me know that since the video of you two has been released, Owen's been experiencing some bullying. Nothing his teacher can't handle, but yesterday was the first time it got physical."

Owen took my distraction as an opportunity to yank away from me and run into the bathroom.

Auntie Shannon got up and looked at me with sympathy. "Apparently, they tied him up with rope in gym class and left him behind the bleachers."

Tears welled up in my eyes. "He's just the sweetest little boy, and this happens because of me."

"You are a good mom. Right now, you could be at some after-party blowing your money. Instead, you have nothing but business on the brain. You're going to get him through this."

I turned and knocked softly on the bathroom door. "Owen, baby, come out. Talk to me."

There was only a loud bag in response.

"Can I try?" Mark asked, standing up.

I closed my eyes and leaned my head against the door. Trying to squelch my anger when I tried the handle and it was locked. Right now he was feeling hopeless and alone. It was an all too familiar feeling for me. One that I would never wish on this sweet boy.

"Mark that is sweet of you, but you should—-"

"Okay," I said, interrupting my aunt. Lifting my eyelids, I wiped at the rushing river of tears. Kicking myself for crying in front of Mark. Hopefully, he just considered this as one desperate mother willing to do anything to help her son. "Sweetie mommies friend is going to talk to you?"

There was only silence in response, so I waved him forward. Even if my aunt looked like she disapproved.

"Hey, I'm Mark," he said, sitting against the wall next to the bathroom door.

"Are you a boxer too?"

Mark's eyes connected with mine. "Not at all."

My hands glided up and down my arms. A cold setting in, that could only be cured by my son's loving embrace.

"How do you know mom?"

My eyes grew wide. Horrified at the route this conversation was taking. I made the kill gesture underneath my neck. He couldn't out me now.

"We dance together sometimes."

The boy laughed. I made a mad dash for the door and tapped on it lightly. "Owen that's——"

Before I knew it, I was being pulled toward the ground. My back was flushed against his chest. His hands covered my mouth. While my mother looked on in stunned silence as if she were witnessing a kidnapping. I tried feebly to break away, to no avail.

"My mom doesn't dance," Owen declared after his chuckles had subsided.

"She does, but just like you, she is embarrassed that people might find out. What she doesn't know and you either, is that when you find something you love, you never deny it. It doesn't matter if it's a person or something as simple as dancing."

He was whispering in my ear now, sending goosebumps down my spine. His closeness reveals the hints of his aftershave. A powerful strength radiating from him in a way that was not threatening, but comforting. This talk wasn't just for Owen, it was for me.

"Being teased sucks."

He slowly lowered his hand from my mouth.

"It does," I acknowledged.

"Sure, but where does it come from. The guy or girls whose envious that they don't have a mom as great as yours. Or they don't have the confidence that you do dancing. There is nothing wrong with either of you. You don't deserve any of this."

"How do you fix it?" Owen mumbled, sounding closer to the door this time.

"You lean on each other. Talk to each other. And you never stop doing what you love. Changing who you are and what you want for someone else only hurts you more."

Surprisingly, the door opens and Owen comes out of the bathroom on his knees. I pull away from Mark's grasp to face Owen. His legs were still draped on either side of me.

"But how do we get rid of the bullies?"

"It's sort of like being on a shaky train. You just got to get through it until you dock at the next station. While doing your best to stay away from harmful situations and people. And when that's not possible just remember to be kind. Bullies are missing something that you have. That doesn't give them permission to hurt you. So if it goes too far, stop it by telling a teacher, principal, or your mom."

Owen looked at me then. "Is that the same thing mom has to do?"

I turned to Mark, genuinely interested in his response.

"She has to be a little more direct with what she wants."

"Because she's an adult?"

His eyes never strayed from mine. "Yes."

Owen then took that moment to launch his lanky, eight-year-old body into my arms. I gasped but took the hug graciously. Kissing the top of his auburn hair as I took in the smell of his coconut shampoo. My close proximity to Mark made this hug a family moment, and that made me more uncomfortable than when it was just me. I craved moments like this for Owen. Yet, I couldn't superimpose Mark into that place like some creepy magazine cutout. But this moment was because of him. "I probably should have told you about my dancing earlier."

"It's okay mom. I'll be your friend and you can tell me all about it," he said.

"Thanks, baby."

He pulled back and looked me dead in the eyes. "I bet you're a really good dancer too."

"She's awesome," Mark chimed in.

"Mark," Owen called, it was clear that he was playing with the word in his head as if he's been given a new toy.

"Owen," he replied excitedly, matching the boy's enthusiasm. Gone was the morose little boy that I had walked in on. Now he was the happy, sunny, kid that I couldn't live without.

Meeting Mark for the very first time.

I stood up quickly and grabbed Owen's hand. Not sure how to proceed with Mark or Owen. They were talking naturally and it was a bit weird. Owen never gets along this well with anyone that I brought home from the boxing world. Not even Farmer. Mark followed my lead and got to his feet as well.

"How can I trust that you're a good dance teacher for my mom?" he asked, dropping my hand and leading Mark back to the couch.

Mark smiled back at me, before allowing Owen to take the lead.

"I think Owen likes him," my aunt whispered, coming up beside him. "You should bring him around more."

I shook my head. "Why? he's not my boyfriend."

She rubbed my arm before walking into the kitchen. The sounds of pots and pans banging around for dinner filled the room.

"Easy, I'll prove it."

Our eyes locked and I'm instantly filled with horror. Dancing in front of my son and auntie was never a possibility. Despite what he said to Owen, I know I'm not that good. But I misjudged the situation. Instead, he launched into the running man. I must've cackled like never before.

"Or the worm," he laughed, worming his way around my living room.

I just shook my head.

"And I don't know what this is, but I can do this too." He was semi-out of breath as he hopped to his feet. Lacing his fingers together, he did a wave-like movement. It was positively horrid.

"I have better moves than that playing, Dance, Dance, Revolution," he said, rolling his eyes. "Mom, where did you find this one?"

I shrugged, snickering behind my hands.

Owen got up and came up to me, whispering, "He's a nice guy, but we've got to talk about his dance skills mom."

"Okay," I whispered back, watching as Owen disappeared back into his room.

Mark approached me with laughter in his eyes. "You'll vouch for me, right? I'm a good dancer."

I brushed some dirt off his jacket. "I've certainly seen you do better."

However, I wasn't the only one with my eyes glued on him. Cooking wasn't that interesting to my aunt. I pulled Mark to the front door. "We can talk a little more in private."

I was actually kind of happy to be alone with him. It's endearing to see how well he got along with Owen. Not only was he good with kids, but he was also light on his feet. And he actually gave me the room, to be honest with my son. Not that Mark couldn't be frustrating too.

"You're kids really cute," he said when we stepped outside.

I leaned against the door jamb. "Thanks."

He nodded. "I meant what I said. You just have to be a little more direct with what you want. Even if that's me gone." He nervously peeled off some of the faded, chipped white paint on the door jamb. "But I'm hoping it's not me."

"It's not," I admitted. "Really."

His smile opened like the floodgates. So bright that I knew I would be able to see it in the dark. We said our goodbyes and I watched him leave. Spending the next 30 minutes convincing myself and my auntie that I didn't want a kiss goodnight. That our chemistry was just leftover dance fairy dust. It wasn't real. The possibility of us wasn't real either.

Chapter 12

We didn't see each other again until Tuesday's mandatory morning practice. Owen's new problems had me switching around my schedule to be home more. So I could be available to pick him up after school. Now I was practicing dance before my workouts. Then hightailing it downstairs before any of the others had arrived. Just to pretend like I had been there the whole time looking slightly less sweaty with fresh socks on.

"Something isn't flowing with these next set of steps. I feel like I need to change it." He dropped my hands and went over to the radio. Tapping on his thighs as he listened intently to the music. Occasionally mumbling to himself and acting out a step.

Every time he brainstormed a new step he tapped his hands against his thighs. It's my favorite thing to watch him do because it's like I'm getting a peek into his creative process. Anyone watching him would find it hard not to crush on his dancing. And admittedly, I had a little crush on him too. Why else would I turn into a bumbling nerd around him? Michelle Nunn was not a nerd. I was the girl that nerds were unreasonably afraid of.

Suddenly, I'm wondering what else is in that head and if he thinks about me as much as I think about him. I imagine him teaching Owen how to woo a girl he likes through the art of dance. He's even doing the tapping during dinner as he tries to decide what to eat. Because he's obviously moved in. And maybe one day, he'll catch me watching him and pull me onto his lap, planting kisses on my cheek. It will quickly turn into a desire for something deeper and a small romp in the bathroom to avoid Owen. But he was out of my league and Owen was my main concern.

I wiped the sweat off my forehead. "Let's just call it a day. It will give you more time to work on it."

"Sure. Oh, I've been meaning to ask how's Owen?"

"He's maintaining. The worst part is being a momma bear and not being able to fix it."

"The easiest answer is also the most difficult. You have to be there to listen. But he has to go through it alone."

I nodded my agreement. "It creates strength of character. Or so I've been told."

He laughed. "I bet you're a hell-raiser during teacher conferences."

I remembered the glares I got this morning at drop off, and the debate's I've missed. "Not really."

"Well, thanks for being here on time. When you said you wanted to switch times, I got kind of worried about you making it here on time or showing up at all."

I shrugged. "No biggie. I've got great follow through."

"Good, because I left an ex over not being on time and canceling plans. It's kind of a pet peeve of mine."

My eyebrows instantly went up at the mention of an ex. "This sounds like an interesting story."

"It's really not," he said, turning back to the radio. "But if you must know—"

"I haven't moved from this spot, have I," I said, genuinely curious about his life.

He pressed paused on the radio and turned back to face me. "So I had this girlfriend that secretly hated when I made plans for date night. Instead, she would ghost me and come up with an excuse as to why she hadn't shown up. Then she would make it up to me by doing the date she wanted in the first place."

I nodded my head from side to side. "And in this age of cell phones, the silence is downright agonizing."

"Tell me about it, I spent so many lonely nights at restaurants and events looking like a complete ass. It also took me too long to become hip to her game. But when I did catch on, I decided to get even. I was just fed up with her penchant for drama and games. So I called one of her frenemies to go out with me. Purely platonic, but I went out to my ex's favorite restaurant. Completely aware that her friend would post the picture evidence on social media. Gloating about how great of a time we had together. To say there was a blow up was an understatement. But I was better off when it was over."

I clapped slowly. "I can't say that I ever agree with being petty, but she definitely played herself. The lengths some girls will go through to get what they want is staggering."

He turned back to the radio and shrugged. "Anyway just don't be late. Now that our classes are in the mornings."

"Okay boss." I stepped out into the hall and smiled pleasantly at the receptionist. She was also in on my little ruse, but I was sure it was only because she had a crush on Mark. I've seen her around in Caliece's small entourage. She was definitely not as sweet or understanding as Sarah who works weekends. If she had to pick her loyalty fell on the side of Caliece's. I walked past the desk and paused at the sound of my name.

"Hey Michelle, I forgot to give you something," Mark said, catching up to me.

I turned to see a small package with a tiny bow on it. The wrapping paper was red with blue balloons. I laughed awkwardly, "It's not my birthday."

"It's just a little something. You can use it for class actually. But it got buried under all my stuff."

I ripped the paper open, feeling like a kid at Christmas. It was a pair of pink and grey, open-toed socks with grippers at the bottom. "Studio wraps?"

"Yeah," he said, pointing to the foot model on the front. "I know that you hate sweaty feet and wet moldy socks. So I brought you something that grips, but is breathable."

I couldn't contain my smile. "You bought me socks."

No one besides Owen had ever been this thoughtful when it came to buying gifts.

He scratched his brow hesitantly. "Yeah, but like, you need them right?"

"Thank you," I laughed, pulling him into a hug.

"No problem, stink bug."

"That's not my new nickname is it?" I groaned.

He smacked his lips as if he could taste the word, putting his arms around her shoulder. "I don't know, I think I kind of like it, stink bug."

I chuckled and pushed him away playfully.

"What's going on here? You got your hand on my girl," Darren bellowed as soon as he entered the building.

Mark threw up his hands before stepping away from me. "Easy man, just joking around."

I grit my teeth. He doesn't want me, but no one else can have me. Once again, I was back in the ice age with his show of machismo. "He just got me a gift. No biggie."

"What kind of gift?" he asked, snatching it from my hand. His entourage laughed behind him like schoolchildren on the playground. But as quickly as he snatched it, he threw it back like hot lava.

"Yeah, she needs socks. She's super fucking anal about that stuff. But how did you know?"

"It got around," Mark replied, holding my gaze a little conspiratorially.

Darren was too busy moving on to his own self-interest to hear the answer. Throwing his arm around my shoulder and leading me back to the gym door. My shoulder slumped as I looked back at Mark. For a second it looked like he was actually jealous, but that couldn't be. Still, I slyly shrugged off Darren's touch. Hoping that Mark caught it as I jogged down the steps with him and his friends. They were going on and on about the dance teachers looking like pussies. However, my mind was back with Mark and the gift he gave me.

There had been so many birthdays and holidays where I've only received what my father wanted me to have. It wasn't until this moment that I realized that I've been holding on to so much hurt because I've missed out on the simplest of affections. The time I spent with Mark was like a salve to old wounds. He made me happy. The only man in my life besides my son who genuinely thinks about me and what I need.

It often felt like being with Darren and being with Mark was like preparing for two vastly different fights. Two men with immensely different skills and considerably different dreams. For the most part, Mark had achieved his and was contented with his outlook on life. Darren seemed to be chasing the inconceivable. A high that was as big as his greatest win.

It's upsetting that a man like Darren gets to brush him aside like a minor annoyance. And replace his arm across my shoulder as if it belonged there. I hated that he looked down on him. Mark was ten times the man he would ever be. But more than hate, I loved the way Mark listened.

The way he touched me sent my hormones into a tailspin. Our almost kiss replayed in my head at the most inopportune times. When we danced together it felt like our body was having their own silent conversation. I loved that he seemed genuinely interested in what was going on with Owen. This all suggested that my crush was turning into something more and I hated that a little bit as well.

Before anything, I needed to think about my needs in the same way that Mark seemed to. Yet, this epiphany hadn't changed my circumstances. My father still had me hanging from a tightrope. Darren continues to feed off my popularity and vice versa, like some flesh-eating parasite.

I know in my heart that I need to get out of their toxic embrace, but Mark helped me realize that this needed to happen now rather than later. For so long my aunt had been telling me that I deserved more. But Mark showed me what that feels like. Our worlds are just two different to meld together, but maybe this could be my starting point. Maybe one day, I could have my own Mark.

However, as long as Darren was in my life I'd never have more than his arms reach. There would never be inspirational pep talks from dad. I'd never get to feel listened to and understood, in the same way, that Mark made me feel all those things and beautiful to boot. My time with Mark exposed everything that I was ignoring.

I'm not going to continue to do that, and forget the cheating. On top of the oppressive nature of our business dealings that touch everything in my life.

And I want to cry because I feel stupid.

I am stupid.

And I've known that for a while, which makes me pathetic too. More than them, I should hate myself.

"What's going on?" My dad asked as he trotted over to us. He gave Darren a hug before nodding to his boys. Looking a little worse for wear as if he had just come off a long binger. But for once, he wasn't my concern, I was.

"Some loser got her some socks."

He nodded as if that made perfect sense. Looking over his shoulder as Darren went over to sign us in at the erected reception desk. I usually paid it no mind. My presence was an announcement. If our newest receptionist wasn't up to date on that, she needed to be. The gym was already packed with huge, sweaty growling men. Like a pack of wolves on the hunt. All of them turned when the alpha and beta walked in. Darren and I were like celebrities. An A-list power couple with merging names like Brangelina. Commanding their attention and respect, but it wasn't Gatorade and I wasn't living for it.

I shoved my gift into my bag. The wrapping paper was still attached. "Dad we need to talk privately."

"I don't need to see the socks," he replied warily. Already rubbing his scraggly beard as he uncapped the water bottle in his hand. The bottle hovered above his lips as if he was afraid of germs. Yet he was a germ, pouring some water into his mouth and taking a swallow.

I almost wanted to laugh.

"No we need to talk about something else," I said. "My bouts for one thing."

He glared at me recapping the drink. A frown wouldn't even be able to explain it, his whole expression was biting. Like he just cut me across the chest with a knife causing me to visibly cringe.

Yet he only led me back into Gideon's office. It concerns me that he has been given carte blanche of the place, but I don't bring it up. Instead, I allow him to close the door behind us. However, when he takes his seat. My inner child squeals like a little bitch and runs away.

"What's about them?" he asked. "I want you to practice as soon as possible. It is good to see you with Darren though. Just listen to me and you'll have a long and happy relationship. Don't nag the man. Let him be."

I nodded. "I agree. I don't want to nag him. I also don't want to be with him."

He stood up, his hands braced against the desk. "We're not talking about that."

I shrugged. "We are, like now, we're in it."

He came around the desk and stood in front of me. Knocking over the nameplate on Gideon's desk. "No."

It was firm but said quietly. Hidden darkness peeking out like a monster under the bed. That one word was overwhelming and struck fear into my heart. Suddenly, I wasn't me. I was a confused 10-year-old me. I rubbed my hands together and scratched my ear with my shoulder. I simply said, "You have to listen."

"Not to garbage," he said stoutly as if I should be declared insane. "He's the best thing to happen to you and your career."

I shook my head. He was getting quieter and I had never seen him like this. Not only was I fidgeting, but it felt like a headache was coming on. And he hadn't even done anything.

"Owen is the best thing to happen to my career."

"Just Owen?"

I nodded. "My hitting Andrew tipped the scales in my favor in a way that nothing else has. But Owen was that shot to the moon. Not Darren."

He was already shaking his head before I had finished my sentence.

"You think some men that smell like leather, beer, and testosterone really give a flying hoot about you and your kid," he frowned.

"Not exactly that way."

"Not at all Michelle. Gideon and I put seats in those chairs because you're dating the hottest attraction on the market. Get your head out of the clouds because it's time you knew that. This ain't about talent. Even if that's the t-shirt that Farmer sells you."

I look down at my hands. The image of Mark smiling back at me as Darren dragged me off gave me strength. Darren would always cheat on me with buxom beauties, and he'd never see me as someone capable of being loved.

"I think—-"

"You think? Because that's your job to make this career happen. You're the person that makes the contracts and seals the deals?"

"No. It's common sense."

He tapped his finger against my temple. Losing his cool. "If you had common sense you wouldn't be cutting off our only means to real money!"

I leaned away from him. "The mistake with Andrew got me in the news. But Owen got me into the hearts of wives and girlfriends everywhere. They finally had something to discuss with their boxing-obsessed husbands and boyfriends. That's what caused the uptake in sales."

"What about Darren? The man loves you," he sneered as if he was finally seeing me and hated what he saw.

"Darren doesn't love me." Attempting to talk some sense into the man without bursting his bubble. He was still my dad, I didn't want to hurt him. So I lowered my voice in the hopes that he would listen to me more. "He hasn't loved me for a long time now. This just may be a business deal to him too. Don't we both deserve to be free?"

He stroked his throat and grimaced. "Just like a woman to jump to the wrong conclusions. What's really going on here? Found out that he's sleeping around on you, have you?"

Shocked, that he knew that Darren was sleeping around on me I fell back into the chair. I knew that they frequently went to parties together, but it never occurred to me that he might see Darren with other girls and say nothing. Complete silence. No warnings. No questions of confusion. No allegiance to his ultra-loyal daughter. My first reaction is to always protect him. A holdover from my time as a child. But I'm not a kid anymore and he's not a father.

He wants me to be unhappy. So he can play the big shot with Darren.

Forget love. There was never any real affection. This whole time I've been tip-toeing around him and this relationship because he's the only parent I've ever known. There are days when I can't even remember mom. How she smelled or what her smile looked like. But no more passes.

Just looking at him was pissing me off. I stood up and confronted him. The chair wobbled behind me. He stood up to his full height, daring me to make a move. Pouring lighter fluid on my anger. But I remembered Auntie Shannon and Owen and everyone who would be disappointed in me. "Darren and I are over."

"You do as I say and it's not by a long shot."

"I'm not a little girl. I'd like to see you make me."

He said nothing. And for once I might have won an argument with my dad. Instead, he reached behind him for a newspaper that had been left on the desk. Pulling off the first page and balling it up. I expected him to throw it at me in a fit. But instead, he leaned down and tried to shove it into my mouth.

"You want to spout off garbage then you can eat it."

He gruffly grabbed the back of my neck, pushing me down into the chair. Shoving the drywall-like taste of the newspaper into my mouth. Trying not to choke, I kicked his knee. He stumbled back and I shot out of the chair like a rocket. Spitting the paper out of my mouth in the process. I wasn't prepared to run, putting some distance between us. Not yet.

"This ain't even about my career. Not even close. I want love. Don't I deserve the kind of love that you had with mom?" I asked angrily, breathing heavily.

He looked at me with a pained expression. "No. You don't. Because you're nothing like your mother! You're just like me. But you can't see it because you've started to believe your own hype. Second to none. Please," he snorted. "Nunn means that you're good for nothing and no one wants you."

"How can you say that? Mom loved you."

He rolled his eyes. "Did she? Because she left!"

I blinked in utter disbelief. My mouth dropped open. "Mom didn't leave. She died. And I don't have the luxury of dying to get away from Darren. So this is over."

I opened the door and stormed back into the gym.

Farmer approached me with a smile that I couldn't return. "Hey girlie, I have been looking for you everywhere. Are we going to practice or not?'

"No! I'm going home," I stormed up the small steps to the ropes. Darren had stolen my time on the mat with one of his sparring partners, again. "Darren?"

His partner saw me first and pointed with his gloved hands towards me. Reluctant to turn around, he tried to get in a few more shots. But did as he was told the more his buddy evaded. "What?"

"We're over." I turned to all the eyes that my statement had drawn. "You heard it here first folks. We're done. Not boyfriend and girlfriend. Completed. But not in a, you completed my life kind of way, but in a, your reign of terror is completed."

Farmer was the only one who appeared to be smiling. When I walked away Darren's curse-word-laced rant filled the air like toxic waste.

Chapter 13

"Yo, Michelle, what's up?" Mark asked, pulling a rather large brown teddy bear out of his trunk. Hitting me with an inquisitive gaze as I tried to hide my face and make a dash across the parking lot. "Is something wrong? I wasn't expecting to see you for the rest of the night."

Sadness settled across my shoulders like an old friend. I couldn't run away from the emptiness that dad felt and gave to me. Not to mention the loneliness of being without Darren. Which felt a lot like being with Darren without the cold stabbing of seeing him with yet another naked chick. Unfortunately, getting from here to the subway without talking about it was, mission impossible.

I just got rid of the greatest burden of my life, but instead of feeling liberated. It felt like a mistake. My eyes roamed up and down the bear in his hand, briefly wondering if there was a different girl besides Caliece that he had his eye on. The secretary perhaps.

"I just got into a fight," I admitted. "Not a physical one, but my dad and I disagree on a lot."

He closed the trunk door and pressed the key fob locking it. Sitting the bear on top of the trunk, he used his knee to hold it in place. It was kind of funny, but my laugh track had died.

"It kind of looks like it took a lot out of you. Like you're tired. I think I've seen that kind of exhaustion before."

I laughed and ran my hands through my hair. Hanging my hands over my neck. "I am exhausted. You're just seeing my rotting soul sprouting roots."

"You're going to need a beer to explain that one aren't you?" Mark picked up the teddy bear and balanced it on his left hip. His eyes lit up as if he had an idea. "Let me take you out tonight. We can talk about your rotting soul...or not."

My eyes roamed back to the teddy bear. The last thing I wanted to do was spend more time drooling over him when he was courting someone else.

His eyes followed my gaze. "Oh no, this is for a woman in my senior class. She'll be turning 90 today. I just took it out now to hide. So I can surprise her later."

"That's sweet."

I leaned back against the car, feeling like I wasn't even capable of holding up my own weight. Just happy that Owen would still be in school by the time I made it home. Maybe Mark was the perfect person to help me get my mind off all of this. However, there was no way I was bearing my soul to my crush. Just so he could see how emotionally unstable I was.

"Don't feel pressured, this doesn't have to be a date. Unless you want it to be. I'm just a good listener and you could use a friend."

"I think I do need that. . . a friend."

"Good." He grinned, before setting the bear back in the car and pulling out his wallet. "I always have at least one of these cards in my wallet because it's my favorite place."

"Venus." I read off the small black and red business card that he handed me. It was a bit mysterious with no descriptive factors. Except for the name scribbled in red raised font on the front. "I only know of the planet."

He laughed, a softness in his eyes as he looked down at me. "Well, this is the club. I want you to meet me there after my class."

"What time is your class over?" I asked straight away.

"Nine pm. But trust me sometimes it's over by 8:30 if there especially cranky."

I sucked in a harsh breath. "I don't know, babysitter and all that."

"Right," he conceded. He searched his pockets for a pen and took back the business card in my hand. Scribbling what looked like his phone number on the back.

It was crazy that I was jealous of a 90-year-old woman and wished the teddy bear was for me. I even had the spot picked out in my living room where I would put it. I've never wanted anything of the sort until it was in his hands. But If I didn't get away from this place the search party would come looking to drag me back. And I wanted to keep talking to him.

"That's my number," Mark said, handing me back the card. His head cocked to the side as I read off the numbers. "You just tell auntie to give me a call if she gives you trouble about babysitting. I heard I can be pretty charming when I want to be."

"Yeah, I don't get time out with the guys or the girls these days. Since the championship bouts, it's just all work. And I still have Owen to think about." I needed to stay level-headed for Owen. At least that's what I told myself because I didn't trust myself with love or even strong like.

"Michelle, think about you. Can you win at life running on empty? You're training for this huge fight and you're focused on your dad, and Owen and only God knows what else. I know when it's a dance competition, I can't focus on anything else. Not even if I'm not getting the moves right. It's like this zen state of being."

Familiarity hit me. "The moment when I step out of my changing room and I put my headphones on. The world is this big loud raging fire, but in my head, it's just me and that song. And I'm straight. On this even keel to the ring."

"You're not going to pull off the biggest upset boxing has ever seen if you're not near that zen spot. And you're not going to stay committed enough to finish your practices with me. You don't have to be in that spot. But you gotta be able to see it on the horizon."

His words made my heart feel like it weighed a ton. I exhaled slowly and tried not to cry, blinking back my tears. "I don't——-"

"Okay. It's okay." He wrapped his arm around me and just held me.

After a while, I pulled away from his embrace. Feeling more composed than when I had walked out. "I might——-"

"No pressure, Michelle. But I'll be there just in case. And I don't know what's going on between you and your dad, but he's a shitty one for making you feel this way. You know, I hate it when you cry. Can balls of iron even cry?"

"I wasn't crying," I said, rolling my eyes.

"No, but your rotting soul was."

I laughed and twirled the card in my hand. "Okay."

This time when I walked away it wasn't with my head down and fear in my body. I actually had a little swing to my hip. And took the steps down to the subway two at a time. Looking forward to convincing my Auntie to watch Owen tonight.

Out of all the people to make me feel better, I certainly never expected it to be Mark. Although, I'd be feeling my father's betrayal long into my sleep. Darren was more than a blip between us. He had somehow found his way into the depths of our relationship. Now it was up to me to figure out if that relationship was still worth saving. I can still feel his hand around my neck as he demanded that I stay with Darren. How can we ever recover from that?

I shouldn't even want to. My dad has always been toxic and it was all I could do not to pass that on to Owen. Looking through my photographic memory I could only remember a handful of times when he wasn't being a jerk. Sadly, all those times included mom. Trips to the amusement park and rolling around in the backyard.

I slid my card and paid for my ride. Running to catch the train that had just rolled up. Making it inside just as the doors closed. An advertisement for a female model with a wide smile brought my thoughts back to Mark. Lost in images of how amazing his smile was when he was holding that silly bear. The arm he had swung around my shoulders was heavy, yet comforting. He was quickly proving himself to be one asshole worth getting into the ring with.

Chapter 14

Auntie Shannon was overly supportive when I told her I was going out with Mark. However, she was reading more into this night out than I was personally ready for. I did just cut ties with the only man I've known since my baby father left. And my dad's voice was no longer dictating my every move. But it was nice having her help me with an outfit. Comparing myself to some of the other girls in line, I'm not sure I would have been able to pull this off without her.

The place was inconspicuous from the outside. If I was passing it on the street it was like any other storefront on the block. If it wasn't for the line I would have missed it completely. Now that I was here, I couldn't help but be a little self-conscious. What if I just looked like a girl playing dress-up? Instead of the young and beautiful look that I was going for. I was still not sure if I could take him ogling a bunch of women at the club. Even if we were just supposed to be friends.

A female bouncer checked all the girls coming in. While a male bouncer checked the men. The guy getting checked across from me was clearly liking the view. I rolled my eyes that the creep could turn a routine check into a sexual encounter worth getting excited about. I thanked the woman and quickly made my way into Venus. That was separated into three rooms. One that was playing salsa music, the other was top 40 and the third seemed to be a themed room. I chose the salsa figuring that was more Mark's style.

Entering the club that was more like a dance floor than a seating area. I navigated the drunk friends, and exorbitant dancers to pick out a spot on the wall. Was this my life now? Back on the dating scene. Dodging creepers and drinking more than I should. Any of it was better than a life deferred with Darren.

I looked over the crowd and spotted Mark at the bar. Instantly I stood up straight and looked over my outfit. My ripped skinny jeans with fishnet stockings underneath perfectly hugged my curves and gave me a sexy edge. Paired with my black lace-up halter top with flounce sleeves. I even threw on a pair of heels, and I hadn't fallen once tonight. Borrowing my aunt's red rose floral heel.

I made my way over to the bar but was stopped midway by the guy who got checked in with me. My eyes darted to the bar where Mark was already living. Did he think I was not going to show?

"Hey cutie, come dance with me? You know salsa. No worries, I'll teach you."

"Sorry, not interested." I went around the guy, but he grabbed my elbow. I dragged in a deep breath. "You don't want me to hurt you."

He must've believed me because he quickly backed up and went on to harass someone else. I caught up with Mark in the entranceway. "Hey."

"Wow," he exclaimed. His eyebrows raised as he looked me over. Some people were coming in, so he guided me to the side. Screaming to be heard over the music that seemed to have been kicked up a notch. "You look great."

He sported his own gray ripped jeans and a loose-fitted white button-up. A leather jacket hung across his broad shoulders.

"You too." The crowd was getting thick and I somehow ended up pressed against him. His hand going protectively around my waist. "I-I don't want to talk."

He took my hand. "Me neither."

Instead, he led me out onto the dance floor. It took a few lessons for me to get the hang of it. But I loved it instantly. The rules were much more freeing than the Viennese Waltz. And we were totally losing track of time.

There was even a moment where it looked like a guy was trying to button in. Dancing closer and closer with each passing beat. But Mark was much smoother than I gave him credit for. He twirled me around until his back was to the guy. I looked up and he was safely between me and the creeper. He never even seemed to be perturbed. It made him appear even sexier. If I had gone with Darren this would have been a whole scene that would have ended with us getting kicked out and the police arriving. That man's ego has no stop button.

Mark pulled me in close and whispered in my ear. "Let's get some air."

I nodded, and he twirled me out in front of him. It was kind of funny because I knew that he was looking at my ass. I was a little flat-chested. So I was glad that I made up for it with my *assets*. I only had my mom's genetics and exercising my glutes to thank. It was nice to know that he appreciated the show. I only changed my dress for this very reason 12 times.

We walked back to the entrance.

"Hey, can we go out for a smoke break?" he asked the bouncer.

"Sure, but you need these blue wristbands to get back in without paying," the bouncer replied, reaching into a small white tray on the ledge behind him. Attaching the wristbands to both our left wrists.

I wasn't aware that Mark smoked. And it was kind of a turn-off. But at least I had a reason to stay away from him now. Kissing an ashtray was never my favorite Tuesday night activity. He took my hand as we pushed through the crowd coming in.

Only standing a few feet away from the door. His back against the side of the brick wall. He pulled out a pack of menthols. I stood across from him and observed him.

"I didn't know you smoked."

He hiked his right leg up on the wall and opened the pack. I almost laughed when he pulled out a piece of gum from the well-used crumpled pack. Shoving it back into his pocket.

"I'm trying to quit." He slapped the back of his right shoulder. "I'm on the patch and everything. This shit has been kicking my ass though. I keep the nicotine gum in my old cigarette pack to try to trick myself."

I completely misjudged him. He was still awesome. And flawed, but prepared to tackle anything with all his might. I was envious of that. "Good luck, I guess. If that's the right thing to say."

He nodded as he watched all the foot track walking into the club. "Good lucks, cool." But when he leveled his gaze on me once more, I almost stepped back. He was so striking. It felt like he already knew everything about me he needed to know. "What's going on with your dad?"

I shrugged. "You don't get to choose your parents. My mom died when I was really little. She went out late one night and got into a car accident. It was fatal. I was the only kid. When I was old enough to understand my auntie explained to me that my dad wanted his first kid to be a boy. Obviously, he wont get that now. But he could if he forced me to play with trucks and get into sports and never wear a dress. In his opinion, she left him, but the icing on the cake was that she left him with a girl."

He pushed himself off the wall and grabbed my hand. But instead of recoiling I just looked at my hand in his.

"Like any little girl, I use to want to be a princess. I was ecstatic when my auntie bought me this yellow Beauty In The Beast dress. He found it and threw it into the big garbage can outside. I spent years trying to hide all the girly toys and clothes she bought me. He became an expert in all my little tricks. My aunt used to get into it with him about it all the time. So the last time, when she brought me a tiara. It was this plastic, rhinestone toy, but to me, it was my crown and the most expensive jewel in the land. I knew exactly where to hide it and keep it. Every night, after he had gone to bed I'd put it on for a couple of hours. And be that girl stuck in the tower with her wicked stepfather. I'd even go to my window and pretend to be talking to my prince. It was the most glorious week of my life. And just like that, it was over. He found it and called me into my bedroom. He berated me for what seemed like forever. Gripping my arm so tight it felt like he might rip them off. Shaking me mercilessly, the pink ribbon in my head unraveled and fell to the ground. I realized then that I wasn't a princess because princesses get rescued and I never would be."

He wiped at the tears falling from my eyes, and I hated that I was crying over a stupid dress and tiara.

"I was only seven. Rebelling was a foreign concept. And once I hit high school there was no point. The person I am was who he wanted me to be. That wasn't some girly girl, but a tomboy who rough houses with the boys and wears t-shirts too big to hide her figure. And today I severed that control in a big way. Except I'm waiting to feel good about it, and instead I feel empty."

He never dropped my hand. Instead, he pulled me closer and wrapped his right arm around my shoulders. Kissing my temple before pulling me into his tight embrace. I appreciated that he didn't respond with some cursory sentimentality. There was no need for one. He just held me. As I inhaled the smell of pears, and lemon minted smoke. I wish that I was more like his type, the fun-loving, giddy girl. Maybe if my mother had lived, I would have.

I pulled out of his grasp. "No more deep shit. Tell me something funny. Any more tails of pettiness hiding underneath that belt."

He laughed and looked down at the growing line at the club door. "I do actually."

I tugged on his jacket and jumped up and down. "Okay spill."

"My fiancee and I were living together."

I tried not to show any visible response to the notion that he was once engaged. Instead, my inner child screamed to high Heaven. Where was this woman? Did he still love her? Had I unknowingly walked into a situation where I had to fight against memories without enough will left.

He lifted his head to the sky and blew a huge bubble with his gum before looking back at me. "Don't worry this was like three years ago."

Looking down at my purse, I blushed. This guy really could read minds sometimes. When our eyes reconnected, his held a twinkling glee.

"She didn't cook. I had to do most of it. Which was never really a problem. Neither was her penchant to steal the leftovers I made for myself to take to work. That's what girls do sometimes. So I let it slide. It was definitely getting annoying. When I would make extras for me and her to have the next day. Yet she would still take the plate that

I made for myself. I don't know if she thought it was cute, but I was pulling teeth."

I didn't say anything. Completely guilty of stealing food off of Owen's father's plate when we were out at restaurants. Although, I didn't think I would be as selfish as to take his lunch bag too.

"One day, my grandmother sent me a small batch of her home-made cookies. I wrote my name on it. I made her promise not to eat them. They were from my granny. She doesn't do it often. So I was kind of cherishing these. It was a small reminder of home, that didn't last one day because she ate them. I didn't get a crumb."

"Well I'm seeing the selfishness, but where does the pettiness come from."

"I waited until she had an important meeting at work. And I sprin-kled the Carolina Reaper, one of the hottest peppers in the world on my food. I heard that lunchtime was interesting for everyone."

I laughed. "You're horrible. But it is just cookies."

His smile faded as he looked off into the distance. "My granny died a month after that. It all made me realize that I loved my fi-ancee more than she loved me. She constantly treated my needs as an afterthought. How can you love someone like that? But I did. The engagement was called off and her stuff was outside the door."

"I'm sorry." My shoulders slumped. "Well, this wasn't very cheer-ful."

He smiled at me. "You know what's going to make us feel better. Theme night."

I scrunched up my nose. "Somehow the word theme seems to en-sure that it wont."

He laughed and walked me back to the door hand in hand. "Give me a chance. I think I know what you might like."

We flashed our blue wristbands to the bouncers. And they moved aside like we were VIPs. Or maybe just two couples in love because he still hadn't relinquished my hand. My face broke out into a huge smile as I heard the 80s music drifting out of the theme room. Maybe he did know what I liked.

"Let's have a drink?" he yelled into my inner ear.

I nodded. He was two for two.

He started a tab and we hung out at the bar. Talking about trivial things. But it felt good to get away from all the heaviness from earlier. And instead, get to know each other through silly questions. Like spirit animals, irrational fears, and my son's favorite color of all things because I don't have one. My face hurt from laughing and smiling up at him so much. I also had a nice buzz to go along with it. The song, In The Heat of The Night by Sandra, was quickly turning into the soundtrack to my evening.

I loved it so much I even started singing to him. In between sips of my, Gin Fizz. My main choice for the night after the bartender recommended that I try it. Yet, Mark didn't cringe at my cheesiness. Or threaten to leave because I'd hit some imaginary limit he deemed appropriate ala Darren. Instead, he joined in. Pulling me on the dance floor by the end of it. The next song already beginning to play.

"I don't know. I think I'm getting a little too tipsy for coherent dance," I laughed, into his ear. Trying to be heard over the DJ.

"It's Head Over Heels by Tears for Fears. You don't need synchronized dance. Just listen."

I swayed from side to side. My hands traced the outline of his chiseled chest to caress his shoulders. He pressed his forehead to mine. As my fingers curled into the hair at the nape of his neck. His touch was already starting to work its own magic on my inhibitions.

My body already craving more of his attention. His singsong voice in my ear caused its own friction between my thighs. When his hand accidentally trailed over my ass, I almost fainted.

"Something happened and I'm—"

I couldn't even let him finish singing. Stealing a kiss. One that would leave an imprint that would haunt my daydreams. But what shot me over the moon was the fact that he returned my passion in equal measure. His lips were soft and inviting. The taste of mint was still on his tongue. Deepening our kiss as if he wanted to possess all of me. The feel of his tongue caressing mine caused trembling in places I wasn't even aware was still alive.

I felt like the luckiest woman in the club. Hoping that he couldn't feel my insecurities rolling around underneath our kiss. For the first time, I found a four-leaf clover in human form. His kiss alone numbed all the parts of my heart that ached and were sewn together with tears.

But was it real?

"Dammit," I said pulling back, chagrined. "Is this that dancing fairy dust again?"

Mark looked at me puzzled until the meaning of my statement dawned on him. He bent down and kissed my cheek softly. "Michelle, this is just us."

I bit my bottom lip. "But I'm not your type."

"I don't think I need my *type* anymore."

"I don't think it's that simple." He bent down to kiss my jawline and I sighed into him. Insecurity taking over my heart. Scared that at any moment he'll realize that I'm not enough. Then I'll miss how he made me feel when he touches me and I'm sent soaring.

"Isn't it? You've drunk nothing, but beer, and today you tried Gin Fizz. Imagine that Caliece and all those girls that surround me are nothing but wine coolers. And today I got a taste of Gin Fizz."

I laughed. "I want to be upset at you and that ridiculous analogy, but I really like Gin Fizz."

He laughed but looked hesitant. "I'm the one that should be mad though, but only at myself. I'm in here kissing a woman already taken."

I quickly shook my head. "No, that's over."

He tried to play it casually, but his voice went up an octave. "Really, since when?"

"Right after I left you. He and my dad have a special relationship. So you can imagine that my decision caused a huge crater in a dam that was already broken."

He looped his finger through my belt loop and pulled me closer. "I'm sorry, stink bug."

"Nothing to be sorry about."

He ran his hand along my midsection. Leaving goosebumps in his wake. "Does that mean you'll let me kiss you now?"

"Whenever you want to."

"Like now," he said brushing his lips across mine. "And now."

He kissed me softly on the lips, before lifting me off the ground. My legs wrapped around his waist. Sinking into the intimate pulse of his kiss. As the music swirled around us like a dust storm.

Chapter 15

We danced all night until the house lights came on. Jetting to the subway before it got too crowded. The platform was dirty but well lit. A CTA worker sat in the booth, crocheting a scarf. But as I looked over at Mark's smiling face I could only be joyful. His cheeks flushed from blinding desire and too much alcohol. And I knew that was what it was because I felt the same way too.

He tapped his bus card on the turnstile and waited for me on the other side as it gave him the green light to go ahead. But as I checked my pockets in all that dancing I must have lost it. I looked up at him wide-eyed.

"I can't find my bus card."

He pulled out his wallet. "Here just use mine."

I frowned. "I'll have to wait 30 minutes."

Time we didn't have if the robotic conductor announcing the approach of a train was correct. The train schedule after 12 pm was notoriously long if we missed this one.

He looked down the steps. "F it."

"What?"

He grabbed my hand and lifted me over the turnstile.

"Hey, get back here!" The worker yelled, coming out of the booth.

We ran down the steps as fast as our feet would allow. My heart pounding in my throat. Another layer of exhilaration added to my skin. The exertion threw my hair back as the train doors opened. "That's not the right one."

"Who cares will get off at the next station and transfer."

We made it inside just as the doors closed. Breathing heavily as if we had just run a half marathon. Our sides split from laughter. The CTA worker threw up her hands as if to say that she doesn't get paid enough. We laughed, into each other's kiss. Getting off two stops away. The platform was empty except for a drunk college student laying across one of the benches. A forgotten radio playing music underneath him.

"I think this may have been the best day of my life," I laughed.

He shook his head. "It's not over yet."

This time when he took my hand, he put my feet to work in a completely different way. Dancing on the platform to, Heart Out by The 1975.

I was pretty sure that after tonight I'd never be able to walk again. Especially in heels. But what a lovely way to die. In the arms of a handsome man, twirling me across a sticky cement floor. My hips swiveled in a motion that would get me disqualified from boxing. I even surprised myself by bending over backward, just in time for him to kick his leg over my head. Before popping up into a side-by-side footwork routine. That left me feeling good about Salsa as my new favorite dance of all time.

By the time our train came, I collapsed in the seat exhausted. Nodding off on his shoulder. Until we had made it to my stop. He was even gentleman enough to walk me home even though it was out of his way.

"You know I can't invite you up. I'm sure Owen and my auntie are already sleeping. But the trouble of you being there in the morning and—"

"Michelle, it's cool."

"I know. I just want you to know that I find you really sexy. But it's just not the time."

He winked at me. "You let me down easy. Now I can tell you, thank you. I know it had to be a big deal telling me about your dad. So, I appreciate you trusting me like that."

"I try not to talk about my relationship with my dad with anyone. Auntie knows, mostly because she was there. But it's just awkward with other people."

My house was a few blocks from the train station. But my feet couldn't possibly take anymore. So I took off my heels and strolled the rest of the way barefoot.

Then I realized that we both were prolonging our walk because it had never taken me this long to reach the end of the block.

"I get what you mean. It's kind of embarrassing for me to talk about mine."

I raised an eyebrow at him. "Now you have to tell me."

He laughed. "My mom was obsessed with advanced mathematics. And when I was little, I had a knack for it too. It was kind of our bonding thing. But every kid grows up. She got more obsessed and I hit puberty. I just wanted to do anything but that."

"You were a nerd?"

"So nerdy. I was teased mercilessly."

"That's why you started working out."

He smiled at me. "It's kind of cliché now, but I wanted to be like the jocks and get the cute cheerleader."

I looked straight ahead. "What would you say to that kid now?"

"You're going to eventually fall in love with dancing. So you might as well take it easy, high school is going to be long for you."

I laughed.

"But getting through it is also worth it."

"Was prom-like your coming out event?"

He looked off as if trying to remember. "It actually was. I wasn't this size, but I was thicker than I was before. I had more confidence. The cheerleader thing didn't happen either. But there was this really sweet girl that gave me my first kiss after a killer dance. It was awesome."

"I kind of wish I could have seen it."

He shrugged.

"I wasn't allowed to go to prom. But I skipped out on my servitude to hang out after. So it was still fun."

"Yeah, my parents have their flaws, but it's nothing like what you went through. They're still alive and generally supportive. It did take them a while to come around to the whole dance thing. But now that I have a resident position and I'm not a ramen-eating pauper. I can call them without them asking me when I'm going to get a new job."

"Are you the only child that they have to harass?"

"I have two sisters that take a lot of the considerable weight off me because they're married with kids. Enough grandkids to keep my parents busy. Does your father absolutely adore Owen?"

"He did in the beginning. The first couple of years after Owen was born, he was my Wikipedia on everything baby. I had never felt closer to him. Even a little jealous of Owen. And I can't even describe it as anything other than. Ohhhh new toy and his attention quickly waned. Owen loved him. But things were noticeably different than before. He exited then Darren came into my life when Owen was about 2."

"So Owen's father is not in his life?"

I shook my head. "No, he wasn't even around to see him born. He had dreams of a different kind."

"Speaking of dreams, outside of being a princess, did you ever want to go to college?"

We hit the last block and all the street lights had gone out. The moonlighting our steps. He offered me his arm and I took it.

"College was always one of those dreams for other people. I spent jr high goofing off and distracting the other kids who were going. It's not as if dad saved me a college fund or anything. His favorite sport is boxing and I think he was kind of grooming me to go in that direction the whole time. I was the only girl on the boy's wrestling team. Pretty good at it too."

I released his arm once I was in front of my building. It occurred to me that he could walk me up, but I didn't want to be any more of a bother. He still had to hop on another train and he had at least an hour to wait. But when I looked at him, I knew he would do anything I asked of him. And it was a heady feeling. He had been staring at me when he thought I wasn't looking. Someone besides Owen actually thought I might be special.

Out of the corner of my eye, three hooded figures were moving towards us quickly. Down the darkened street. But by the time it dawned on me what was happening it was too late.

"Give us all your money and jewelry?" He barked shakily, pointing a gun at us through his pocket.

A wisp of dirty blond hair poked out underneath the navy blue rusted jacket. The thief's eyes were red-rimmed and bloodshot. Santa

Clause could find every house in Antarctica with how red his nose was. His companions looked a little soberer but just as unhinged. The second companion's face was filled with sores and pox marks. A third smaller, more female frame, stood out of the light cast by the door. Obscuring her face like a nightmare out of a Japanese horror movie.

"Everyone be cool. I'm going for my wallet," Mark said, moving slightly so that he blocked me from the others. Pulling out his wallet, he tossed it at the feet of the man with the pistol. "We don't have anything else."

"No," I croaked over his shoulder. Concerned that this could all be a false alarm. That guy didn't appear to have a gun. However, I'd never risk my life or his on it. Instead, I said a silent prayer that we would both leave this unharmed. We were still outnumbered.

"I want her shoes." The quiet woman declared reaching behind Mark to snatch them from me.

Purely on reflex, I reeled back and hit the little monster in the jaw. This started a domino effect of the two males ganging up on Mark. However, I was impressed that he was holding his own. I was not much help because this woman had developed the strength of she-hulk for a pair of shoes. So I used gravity to my advantage and simply stopped pulling. She lost balance and hit the curb hard. Hitting her chin on the concrete and spilling some teeth and blood on the asphalt. She was crying like a newborn.

It allowed me enough time to help Mark. I hit the biggest one below the belt. Sending him to his knees with a throat punch. That would have him missing his Adam's apple. The ring leader who had yet to produce a gun was already in a sleeper hold in Mark's arms. Passing out only seconds later. The other two took off running without him.

I got us safely behind the automatic locks of my building. Allowing Mark to pull me into a hug. Finding comfort there. In a blink of an eye, Owen could have been without a mother. The very thought was scary.

"You okay?" he asked, looking me over.

I nodded, but I wasn't. And from his grip on me, he knew that too. Maybe it was better if he stayed.

Chapter 16

Mark ended up sleeping over at my house. I snuck him out, past a snoring auntie and a sleepwalking kid. It sometimes felt like I was the sleuth from that old Madtv cartoon. Slinking against the wall, I pressed my body up against it so hard that I could be the wallpaper. Just surprised that the hoopla downstairs with the police car hadn't woken either of them.

By the time the cops arrived, all of our assailants had run away. But the cops assured me that if their injuries were true then they would be showing up at a hospital soon. When they took photos of the injuries on my hand I felt a little like a criminal. And this nightmare was still not over because I had to go in and make a proper statement.

One of the cops recognized me. But for some reason that didn't make me feel any better. This wasn't about my career. Owen could have been without a mother. My career may have been the reason that we had a fighting chance. But, it was Mark's bravery that I leaned on.

Once, we were safely behind the locked doors of my bedroom, I learned that this wasn't Mark's first brush with the criminal element. Someone had stolen a family heirloom from Caliece to sell. He ended up tracking the guy down and beating the crap out of him just to get it back.

Something about that story reminded me of my own pseudo brush with heroism. I ended up revealing my own history in High school when I hit this particular douche guy. Mark made a joke about violence not being the answer for Owen's sake. Of course, Owen was always a completely different story. I wanted him to grow up in a home of love and acceptance, where acting out was not necessary. Regardless of the motives behind it.

We stayed up into the night talking about our lives and my hopes for Owen. In a way that I had never had before with anyone. But I had another fight the next day. So I set my alarm ridiculously early. Intent on getting him back through the door unseen. Without any of the questions that I wasn't prepared to answer.

Luckily, my auntie only stirred on the couch but doesn't open her eyes. Unable to breathe until I got Mark outside the door. Closing it gently behind me.

"Michelle, I think that's the best floor I've ever slept on, stink bug," Mark said, his eyes roaming over my body like I was a snack. "You've got to invite me to do it again."

I couldn't be imagining how my body was responding to him. Inhaling a steady breath, as a poor attempt to control my breathing. Our attraction to each other is as constant as gravity and the round shape of the Earth. Except, I've never been certain about anything outside of Owen. Yet, I'm certain that my heart wants him to be closer.

You never know the outcome of a fight and love is the same way. But the harder you work at it the easier it becomes to predict. And my heart that had solely been trapped behind the ropes is finally meeting its match.

I smirked, "really?"

"Yeah, that purple duvet from my view of the floor up was the moon dust to my dreams," Mark said, grabbing my waist and pulling me closer.

I just looked at him and laughed. He's so cute when he's flirting. Oddly, I wanted to fix him a healthy breakfast. Demand that he stay and watch him eat, but I could never voice that aloud. What would it look like If Owen was staring at a strange man at the breakfast table? Heck, what would he think? Have breakfast with me and my kid and auntie. I'll fix you egg whites. As much as I wanted to be his, I couldn't right now.

I spun around, not sure if I heard movement on the other side of the door or not. "You've got to go now," I said turning back to him. "I'm not going to be able to attend rehearsal at all today. I have a fight tonight. That means I have to work on my agility training today." I bit my lower lip, keeping one hand on the doorknob. So I could feel if anyone opened it. "But I did enjoy our time together. Before and after, my shoes were almost taken."

"Don't think about it." This time Mark isn't smiling. He knows how badly the thought of dying on the street affected me. I know that my auntie would likely step up if she had to. But no one can replace mama. I knew that better than anyone.

"I'll try not to," I said softly. "Owen certainly can't find out. He's already concerned about me because of boxing. I don't think he needs to worry about me walking down the street too."

He brushed his hand across my cheek and nodded. "If you need anything big or little. Don't hesitate to call me. I'll even go down to the police station with you. My badass shouldn't be worried about anything."

I smiled bashfully. "I think my daredevil did a good job of making sure that I have nothing to worry about."

Giddy, was exactly how I felt when our lips touched for the second time since the incident. It was as if Darren, my dad, and boxing had been completely washed away and the only thing left was two people who happened to like each other. There was no sin or guilt in that and it was liberating. Our lips softly parted.

Our hands lingered a bit longer, not wanting to sever our connection. An unspeakable link drawing our heads together.

"Listen," Mark began, "How about I come to your match tonight? I haven't been since you decked Andrew."

"You will probably enjoy it much better. Once the violence isn't so much in your face," I laughed. Understanding, just how much of a mistake that show of bravado was.

"Then it's a plan."

Watching him leave felt bad, like a stomach ache. Like he was taking a piece of me with him. I opened the door, only to walk dead into my auntie. She's simply grinning. I've obviously been had, but there was no Owen. So this wasn't a complete failure. "Hi."

She hit me playfully on the arm. "Good morning to you too, lucky girl!"

I ignored her and opened the door to the bathroom. Intending to take a shower before I needed to be at the gym. But all she does is follow up behind me. Resting in the door jamb, clearly waiting for answers. But how honest did I have to be about everything that happened last night? There was still the matter of the huge pink police car in the room. Yet, what I wanted to hide was everything that I had gone through with Mark. I wasn't ready to share him with the world. "Something happened last night."

She rolled her eyes and threw her head back. "Can we skip the part where I looked through the peephole to see who you were talking to?" she said. "Because from the looks of it that date went realllly well."

I bit my lip. Sitting on the side of the tub and testing the temperature of the water with my hand. "It did," I replied, measuring my words in order to not freak her out. "But that's not what I want to talk about."

She laughed and then turned around to face the other way. "I know that it's super embarrassing to talk about this stuff with your aunt. So I'm going to turn around and you can pretend I'm not here. That way you can give me all the delicious detail without me staring you down."

It was silly, but I found myself taking her up on the offer. "Getting ready yesterday for our non-date was stressful enough. But inviting him upstairs was like another level of uber stress. I didn't know if he had some picture of me in his head and if seeing my room would somehow ruin that. Then there was the ever-present you know what in the air. Which we didn't do, not that you asked."

"You mean to tell me, you didn't sleep with him," she said, positively aghast as she turned to face me. If I didn't know any better I would think that she was disappointed.

"It was our first non-date," I laughed. "Why would I do that? Why would I do that with Owen down the hall."

"Many parents manage to make it work," she huffed, with a shake of her head.

"It will happen in its own time." Not that I wasn't tempted last night. It got a little hot in my room and Mark was forced to take off his shirt. My heart went into palpations. All I wanted was for him to lower that lean physique across my bed, and lean back as I slowly devoured him. But I'm not the most experienced person in the boudoir. I haven't had anyone in my bed since Owen's father left.

If I'm going to take someone into my confidence again, it's not going to be some casual fling. "Besides that's not the only thing that happened last night."

"Don't tell me that he didn't want to?"

I grabbed her hand and took her over to the couch. Opting to sit on the edge of the couch. I had to play this one cool. "That's not what I mean. Auntie, last night I was robbed or almost robbed."

She turned around and came to my side. "What the hell happened?"

I rubbed my forehead. The worried lines on her forehead increased in size with my every word. "Some drug addicts came upon me and Mark last night outside the building. We managed to fight them off. I got one good and Mark got one. Once we were safely out of harm's way, I called the cops. They're trying to track them down as we speak. Hopefully."

She was so quiet that for a moment, I thought I had sent her into a diabetic coma. "All this happened in front of the building."

I nodded.

"And you and Mark had to fight for your lives," she repeated. "Is Owen safe here?"

I grit my teeth, not sure I appreciated where this was going. "Owen is safe wherever his mother is. We were out late at night into the morning and that's not a situation that Owen would be in."

She looked at me over her eyelashes. "Yes, but you know that my neighborhood is a lot safer." I grimaced, knowing that my auntie was about to cross the line between concerned relative and parent. "You need to live in a building where the landlord actually cares. The kitchen would also be bigger than a broom closet. Owen might even be able to have his own bathroom. If you think about it, I might be able to put in a good word at my building."

My heartbeat raced as I reminded myself that I loved this woman. "I will think about moving. After my prepaid lease is up here. As of now, I'm content with my decision, and so is Owen."

She hedged a bit. "Sure, but what happened to you must have shed some light on how dire things are."

I pulled my hair back into a ponytail, grabbing a hair tie from out of the bathroom cabinet. "It shined a light on how awesome Mark was. Crime being everywhere has never been worth giving yourself ulcers about. You should think about that on the other side of the door."

Luckily, she left without me having to push her out. Walking swiftly out the door as if I had insulted her honor.

Closing the door, I appreciated the time alone to mull over everything that happened.

That robbery had been a completely random event, and out of character for the neighborhood that I had grown to love. However, if it hadn't been for this scary moment, I never would have invited Mark upstairs. And I never would have solidified the relationship that I was now sure that I wanted with him. Mark pulled me to him when we said our goodbyes. My heart melted in the best way.

He knew pretty early on that he was sleeping on the floor when I pulled out the pillows and blankets and rested them there. But he just cracked jokes about it in order to make me feel better about it. Only for me to end up sleeping at the foot of my bed so that I could see him better as we talked. The butterflies kicked up in my stomach as it dawned on me that for once I may have bagged a good one.

"Hey," my aunt said, knocking briskly on the door. "Ms. Know-it-all remembered that Owen has another debate tonight after her fight."

"Shit," I said underneath my breath. "Yes, I totally remembered."

The last part was much louder.

I stared at my reflection in the mirror for several seconds. "Today isn't going to go well at all, is it?"

"Stay focused," Farmer instructed me. "You've been distracted lately, but out on that mat I need you listening to me."

I grunted in agreement. Trying to shake off the nerves as I jumped rope. I'm supposed to be saving all my energy for the match. But this was my first one without my dad or Darren in the stands cheering me on. They were a bunch of shits, but I felt their absence in a really weird way. I kind of felt like I couldn't do this without them.

Rehearsal had been a virtual ghost town. At least that's how it felt without their larger-than-life personalities looming over my shoulder. Keith just enjoyed my suddenly renewed commitment to practice without the distractions. Which ought to be an everyday thing. And he more than got me ready for my fifth fight. So I was worrying for nothing.

By the time I heard a knock on the changing room, I had managed to cool down.

This changing room was nothing, but lockers. The woman's area, I suspected. Several rows of beat-up black metal lockers took up every available space in the rather large room. The walls not containing lockers were positively bare and looked like it could use a fresh coat of paint. But I ignored everything and stayed focused on my opponent tonight. Not even bothering to pay attention when Farmer went over to open the door. That was blocked from view by a set of lockers. I stopped jumping and handed Keith the rope.

"Is it okay if I talk to Michelle?"

Mark's voice drifted over to me through the black metal lockers. He was here. In my changing room. I went over to sit on the bench, feeling a bit anxious. I knew he might come. But it was one thing to imagine him as a nameless face in the crowd; it was quite another for him to see me decked out like a sweaty boy.

It didn't help that I was wearing a pair of shorts that could double as parachute pants. He certainly has seen me in a sports bra before, but this particular combination was not flattering. Even if he wasn't dating Caliece, women like her were definitely his type. It was foolish of me to think that he wouldn't be comparing them to me. Touching my boxer braids, self consciously.

"Hi there," he said reaching out to shake Keith's hand. Before stuffing his hands back in his pockets. "Do you think I could get a moment alone with her guys?"

"Keith, this is the friend of the guy Michelle hit, remember?"

I had barely looked at him since he walked in. But Farmer's little declaration caused us both to look at him sternly.

"Yup," Keith nodded, pointing as if it was all too clear.

"I apologized for that," I replied under my breath. I felt like a kid who was about to be embarrassed by her overbearing parents. Farmer was about to launch into the what are your intentions with my daughter speech. While Keith was prepared to kick him out, Fresh

Prince of Bel-Air style. Farmer sounded suspicious of the whole situation. Which is better than him knowing the truth about what was going on between me and Mark. I didn't have any reason to believe that he wouldn't support me, but the fewer people that knew the better.

"If you're here to cause trouble don't bother."

With a quick glimpse at Farmer, he said, "I just want to let bygones be bygones. We sort of have an understanding already. But what better way to end this than where it started."

Farmer rose to his full height and practically stared me down. A subtle quiet to his actions that made it hard for me to read him. "I don't want you to get hurt."

"I'm not going to hurt him."

"It's not him I'm thinking about. Keith and I will be right outside the door." He pointed at Mark. "Hey, there's a lot riding on this fight. Keep your distance."

"Yeah, she's already worn herself out jumping rope," Keith said, in disbelief as he sauntered off.

Laughing to myself, I settled back on the bench.

"Seeing you back here. It kind of puts a new spin on this whole thing. I got lots of respect for what you put your body through."

"Thanks," I said unable to communicate just how much his saying that means to me. So outside of feeling like a dude, I felt like a bumbling ogre.

"I get a little closer to understanding you every day and I like you more and more. And I kind of feel like this kid who's discovered a new toy and I don't want to share."

I thought about making a joke about toys, but stopped because I felt like something important was happening here and I didn't want to miss it. He was at my match, backstage no less, and he didn't have to be. So at least on some level, I knew that he cared. And he's admitting openly, in a way no man has before, that he does. Darren could never be this open and honest with his feelings.

"But I do have to share you. I can't demand your time because you're this fire mom. I don't think I could even demand your attention if I wanted to, because the people in those stands would riot. But I'd be stupid not to admit that what I want now is you. So if being with you, means that I have to accept whatever slot you can fit me in. I'm cool with that because you're totally worth it."

I stared down at my wrapped hands, feeling unworthy of this man that had found his way into my life. "A part of me wants to ignore everything you're saying. Only because pretending like you're feelings aren't real would just be easier for me. But I look forward to seeing you every day. Your presence has staked its claim and now my life feels a little empty without you. It's one of my unavoidable truths."

"I never expected this for us. But I find myself missing your laugh. Or pondering something you've said to me long after you're gone. And I get why I can't be yours. We're literally and figuratively on opposite sides of the same field. But I'm gonna shoot my shot anyway. My feelings were not just some drunken adrenaline haze there still in here," he said, pointing to his chest.

His words finally draw my eyes to him. I know that pretty soon this love fest will be broken up by some pretty demanding dudes. So I'm trying to come up with something poignant to say in a quick sound bite. But the truth of his words wont allow me to be so trivial. His words to me last night were replaying in my head and my heart.

"We're really going to do this then?" He sealed his response with a kiss. I was finally happy. Little sparks of joy were firing off in my head and it felt good being this close to him. How could two people so opposite in nature and career find so much love and concern for each other?

Chapter 17

I hear my phone vibrating and I reluctantly break the kiss. "Hold on, I have to get that."

After a five-minute search for my phone. I pull up a calendar reminder on my phone. Gasping as it reminded me that Owen's second debate was tonight. "Shit."

My cursing draws his eyes. And I love how concerned he looks instead of being put off that I'm not perfectly coiffed. He beckoned for me to rejoin him on the bench. "What's the matter?"

"I just got some more motivation to end this fight earlier. Which will more than likely have the opposite effect."

He takes my phone out of my hand and reads the announcement quickly. It's not as if it's his problem. He'll probably fly the coop like everyone else after the fight is over. I needed to worry about finding a ride.

"I didn't know that Owen liked to debate," he commented, sounding genuinely impressed.

"It's a new development," I replied, my voice devoid of the confidence that had been there only moments before. Returning my phone to the bag in my locker.

"You getting there on time wont be a problem. I'll just drive you."

I barely nodded, finding it hard to believe that he would even offer. Owen had always been my problem or my concern depending on which men you asked. Mark wasn't even his child, so I don't even have the right to ask for him to take time out of his evening like that.

"I can't ask you to do that," I said, my voice tight and controlled.

"You can, and I'm offering," he said casually.

I'm doing a little dance on the inside, trying to remain as cool as a cucumber on the outside. Partly because I knew that if I miss this on top of everything else, it was going to hurt Owen beyond repair. And partly because my own father would never dare. Win or lose my father had plans at someone's after-party. Family life ended when I turned 18. Of course, I entertained the idea of Darren being a part of my family, it was never a reality.

"Maybe, I could even take you guys out for a late dinner after? As long as it's okay with mom."

"Don't you have plans already? Or some client that needs to see you?" I'm eyeing him as if he grew a third eye and I know I look crazy, but I can't help it.

He grabbed my hands and held them between his. Turning so that his whole body was facing me. "Michelle, you're what I care about. If you need a ride and I'm free it's a no-brainer. I'd love to spend the rest of my evening with you and Owen."

"It's just that for many, Owen is an afterthought," I said quietly. "And I don't expect you to be an automatic father. So if you're not feeling this. Don't start it."

"Being a father isn't a dream that keeps me up at night," he said, honestly. "But I see it in my future. And if being with you means that the future is sooner rather than later. I'm cool with that. No excuses here. I'm going into this with my eyes open. But tonight is just dinner and some support. It's not hard to figure out from your reaction that you didn't actually plan for his event."

My heart plummeted the same way it did when I walked into that school and realized that I was late. Pulling away from him to bury my face in my hands. Closing my eyes as if it was enough to blind me from all my faults. Mark volunteering to help me meant the world, but it also highlighted that I too was guilty of using Owen as an afterthought. Owen was honest and good, and he only deserved my best.

He pulled my hands away from my face as if he understood perfectly. "You're doing the best you can as a mom. Don't be too harsh on yourself. Showing up is what matters."

"I tried telling myself that, but if I don't get there on time," I shook my head, unable to finish the sentence.

"I never considered myself a speed demon, but for tonight I'll put in my application for Nascar. You can trust me to get you there."

I laughed. "Well wait, don't go getting any tickets on my account."

"It is my pleasure," he replied firmly. "I'd just put it on your tab."

"There's a tab?" I asked, raising an eyebrow at him.

"Of course, and all these free dance classes are on it," he said, teasingly, giving me a wink.

My mouth dropped open and I squinted at him. "You're a slick one."

A knock came at the door then. "Conversations over. Second to none is needed on her dance floor."

Mark stood up at that point and looked me straight in the eye. "It's cool, I think we understand each other now."

I had to shove my emotions down like they never existed just to keep myself from reaching out to kiss him. Keeping a cool aloofness about me as Keith eyed us with suspicion. Farmer was already out on the mat so he wasn't picking up on anything.

I didn't even want to go to the fight. That's how I knew without a doubt that I don't miss Darren. He never really gave me anything to miss. It's not like I wanted to be dragged to another party with complete strangers. The problem was, he never even entered my mind when I was with Mark. Maybe he was getting under my skin quicker than I was ready.

He lies without a second thought over the nature of our conversation with Farmer and Keith. That decision was hard to swallow but necessary. Even as I traipsed down the aisle to the ring, I imagined myself going on a walk with Mark and I'm not even a walk kind of person.

However, when I stepped into the ring, a switch flipped. The only thing I was imagining was the girl across from me telling me that I wasn't good enough. That I was a simple fad that Mark would grow bored with, and it helped me put my game face on.

Not only did I develop the courage to leave Darren.

I had a cool boyfriend who was the complete opposite.

I had never been this lucky in life and fully expected to lose this fight. If only because too many things were going right in my life and something had to give. The woman across from me had been staring at me with cold contempt. So if anyone was going to ruin my streak it was her. Instead, I focused on Farmer and Keith's advice and put the rest behind me.

We touched gloves and my fifth fight had begun.

But it didn't take long to catch on to this girl's deal. She wasn't used to thinking on her feet and was copying my stance. Okay, parrot. Let me switch things up a bit. I dipped down and missed a shot coming straight for my head. Coming up to hit her in her stomach.

Her cowardliness only enhanced my need to win.

For ten rounds we came out of the corner swinging. Hitting each other in the midsection. But the grimace on my face wasn't of pain, but anger. She was in the way of my championship, and she didn't deserve the opportunity. I grit my teeth and refocused. This time when I swung it sent her back into the ropes and over the edge. The referee counted while her cutter went over to make sure that she was okay. I won by default because it was clear that she wasn't getting up.

But my win wasn't because I was lucky. No, I was starting to realize that this was meant to be. My jaw was aching and I had a killer headache. I would need a deep tissue massage and an ice bath for the next couple of days. Farmer would be cracking down more on my time and there would be no time for excuses.

It didn't matter how hard I had worked to get here; all that mattered was how much further he had to pull me. Our need to win was suddenly bigger than my desire to do so. I could always listen to my desire and walk away. But I couldn't do that with ambition.

Ambition required untold sacrifices.

I just had the feeling that my bill was going to be expensive.

I matched his long strides to the door with my frantic ones. For the first time, I might actually make it to one of Owen's events on time. Auntie Shannon was texting me the whole ride over that it starts at eight pm. It was now 7:59. If it wasn't for Mark, I wouldn't have made it this far. I'd still be home, just jumping out of the shower. Now, no one would be looking at me as if I had won an award for worst mother ever.

More importantly, I would be able to make Owen proud. The knowledge that Auntie Shannon was saving two spots for us also drew a smile from my lips.

"I think we managed to just make it."

"I'll never be able to thank you enough," I whispered to him, as a teacher I didn't recognize greeted us at the auditorium door.

"Go right on in."

"You made it. I'm so glad." Auntie Shannon whispered, before leaning over to shake Mark's hand.

The lights were turned down and the door to the auditorium closed. The outside frame of the stage looked like a castle. Clapping enthusiastically, as puke-green velvet curtains were pulled back revealing Owen's debate teacher sitting in between two students. She approached the podium set up in front and cleared her throat.

"Hello, parents, teachers, and students. I'm Mrs. Coyne and welcome to our second debate. Our after-school team has practiced diligently since the inception of this program. Honing their communication skills and overcoming their fear of speaking in public. Every one of those students was worthy of standing before you today. However, Owen Nunn and Posie Jacks had the most convincing, but hilarious arguments on the subject of love. Please give Owen Nunn, a round of applause as he presents the case, For Love."

A lot of students started whistling and clapping and I wondered if the school made it mandatory for all 5th and 6th graders to attend. Looking at a large number of kids with their parents. But I was more impressed with the fanfare they were giving Owen. Perhaps the stigma of that video was behind him.

"Good evening, everyone."

I nearly squealed at how proper he was being. The picture of adorableness. Barely able to reach the top of the podium as his teacher rushed off stage and returned with a step stool. Adjusting the microphone as he put his notes on top of the walnut podium.

"Love is food for your spirit. It's the only thing that God gives and expects to receive in return. A perfect love. In life, Love is the only thing that we chase down with enthusiasm. For example, the teenage boy who lives in my building was literally chasing down love when he saw his girlfriend leaving with his friend."

This statement elicited chuckles from the parents.

"Some might say that is an argument for the opposing team. However, for a little while, he was important to someone. He knew what it was like to give love and receive it. And that is the best gift of all. Even if it's one of those things that you don't get to keep for long. Like when you go to the museum and can't touch anything because everything is rare. When you suddenly have love, it makes you feel invincible like a superhero."

One of the mothers in front of me said, "awww."

I looked over at Auntie Shannon and smiled. Our boy was doing good.

"I'd like to be a superhero even for a little while. Mothers are superheroes. Their love for their kid is the most magical thing ever. I've got a little of that magic in my life because my momma loves me."

Mark reached over and squeezed my hand. But I kept my eyes trained forward trying not to tear up.

"But the lack of that mommy love in other kid's lives can turn them into bullies. I almost turned away my mommy's love because I was worried about bullies. But a family friend helped me realize that love is a cure-all. You grab on to the people who love you the most because they can get you through tough times. In the words of my grandpa, life is one big tough time. Wouldn't it be miserable not to have loved throughout it? Thank you."

He stepped down from the podium and stood on the side to bow.

I stood up and clapped as if my life depended on it. Not concerned that we were the only ones giving him a standing ovation. He listened. He listened to me and Mark and even grandpa. Although, that last one gave me pause. I was just astonished that I hadn't completely turned him into a maladjusted kid from the violence in my career. He gets it all, and he's still an awesome fluff ball of love.

"Thank you, Owen. Now I introduce to you, Posie Jacks, presenting the case, Against Love."

An adorable pigtailed blond girl, with a white and black polka dot dress, approached the podium. "Guys suck and boys drool. It's an old childhood rhyme, but is it true."

You could tell from her walk that this girl was all sass. But the first words out of her mouth confirmed it. This was definitely going to be fun.

It was clear by the end of her speech that this girl had managed to get people to root against love. Or men depending on whom you asked. But I was biased and Owen would always be my winner. I was shining love on him much to his embarrassment all throughout our late ice cream run with Mark and Auntie Shannon. After he made it known that he already had dinner. My cheeks positively hurt from all the smiling as I watched him interacting with Mark in the car.

He looked genuinely upset when they had to part ways back at the house. I tucked him in and went back downstairs to say goodbye to Mark.

"I wouldn't have made it without you."

"It's no big deal."

I shook my head. "But it is. Even my own father found these things...hard to attend. Darren just thought that everything that didn't involve him was unimportant."

"I like the kid and I think it's cool that I could be here." He grabbed my hand.

I patted the top of his hand. "But it's more than that for me. I was on the heels of another win. My first fight in the series and all I asked everyone to do was help me see my son's debate. And no one would help me."

His brows furrowed. "I'm sorry."

"I was late and I tried so hard. Of course, he hated me for a little while after that."

"I think you more than made up for it tonight." He looked at me shyly. "Want to go for a walk?"

I looked back at the building door thinking about the last time we had taken a walk in this neighborhood. But I never let fear lead me. Besides, whoever it was I was sure we could take them. "Sure."

We ended up walking to a nearby park that was just 10 minutes from the house. Claiming the closest bench as our own. Looking out over the empty grassy knoll that was perfectly maintained. The playground was absent of children's laughter as the swing swung back and forth in the breeze.

"You look beautiful tonight by the way."

I looked down at my plain white tank top and peplum patterned pants. Something that I had thrown on to be quick about it. When I was just concerned with making Owen's debate. "I looked better during the first debate. I even wore a dress."

He laughed into his fist. "An actual dress? When will I get to see this miracle."

"Day before the competition. Maybe?" I teased.

He raised an eyebrow at me. "You're beautiful in everything you wear."

"Not at all, my auntie has more style than I do."

I played in the dirt with my sandals. Drawing a heart with the tip of my shoe. My black elastic-banded flats were reminiscent of my hand wraps in boxing. The only reason I had felt comfortable buying them. But they were little defense against the dust I was kicking up.

He grabbed my left hand and traced the lines on my palm all the way up to my fingertips. Goosebumps traveled up my arm. An instant craving for him to touch me somewhere else. Holding my breath as he sprinkled light kisses across my tips. Tangling his other hand in my hair. That on this rare occasion was down around my shoulders and not in a ponytail. I never thought that I'd enjoy someone playing in my hair. Leaning into the hand that brushed across my cheek. I kissed his palm lightly.

"What are you thinking?" he asked. He trailed his thumb over my chin and up to my lips.

"Nothing," I said proudly. "I don't have a to-do list when I'm with you."

"I do feel like a superhero when I'm with you. Like the world saw fit to trust me with something special. A woman whose literally a force to be reckoned with."

His words left me at a loss. I knew that everyone that entered my life was there for a season and a reason. Darren taught me the value of sticking up for myself. My first love gave birth to my lasting love, Owen. Now I'm with Mark and our relationship hasn't exactly reached fruition yet. So I might be a little premature but I think Mark's here to teach me about real love. It's not even a question anymore. I do love him. "You are my superhero."

I hopped on top of him without a second thought. Kissing him as if I were drinking straight from a well.

He broke our kiss and laughed, "You really want to do this here?"

"I thought you could handle anything?" Searching his eyes for signs of doubt.

"You know I can."

He nipped at my bottom lip sending thrills down my spine that could not be attributed to just the breeze. His hands grabbed me about the waist, pinning our bodies together as if we needed each other to breathe. Fingertips digging into my flesh as if he wanted to imprint on my very soul. But I was no delicate flower and I could handle him if he could handle me. There was nothing he could do to hurt me.

His tongue probed the inside of my mouth like a skilled architect. Mapping out the corners of my pleasure centers. I should be worried about getting caught by the police or some random passerby, but he was kissing away all my doubt. I wanted this moment. And I wanted it with him.

His fingers dipped under the stretch band of my pants to probe my center through my cotton panties. Swallowing my moans with his kiss. Leaving me whimpering, when he broke our kiss to leave rough kisses down my neck.

I wanted to be wearing a dress right now so bad. The length of him pressed against my thigh. Pushing against his magical fingers as he caused the rolling butterflies in my stomach to tremble. Bracing myself against his shoulders fully intending to hang on for dear life. A moistness seeping through my panties to the point that they were probably translucent.

I felt completely safe in his arms as if we were in a five-star hotel with silk sheets instead of a park bench underneath a Buckthorn tree.

"Take it off," he barked, his voice full of need.

I stood up and shimmied out of my pants. Throwing them at his head. Watching as he dug into his pocket for a condom. Before I went for my panties.

"Keep those on I'll work around it." He twirled my pants like a rope and used it to pull me back onto his lap. "Did anyone ever tell you that you look gorgeous in just some panties and a tee?"

"It seems to be a new development," I said, kissing him between every word. In awe of the pure brawn that I had wrapped around my fingertips. His grunt of need music to my ears. I took his lips between mine our molten hot kiss raising the temperature on the bench. Barely aware of the pain as my knees dug into the wood. Helping him unzip his pants as he shielded my backside from the world with mine. Moaning as my moist center pulsated with want. Begging for his fingers to return as I grinded against him.

"Pull it out," he commanded, cradling my face.

I pulled against his boxers. His engorged flesh fell into my hand. Staring into his eyes as I put it in. My head rolled back as his hands went back around my waist. He hammered me with raw abandon. I gripped the wood backrest on either side of him. Until I released a primal scream that I muffled in his neck. His thunderous warmth filled me soon after. But there was no time to bask in the afterglow. I slowly stood up and put back on my pants. Both of us were breathing hard as if we had just run laps around the track.

"I can't believe you weren't scared of getting in trouble?" He asked, standing up and buttoning his pants.

"Of course not, being with me means a walk on the wild side Mark." That sounded way more confident than I felt. Because reality was setting in and I was getting anxious. "Let's get out of this park."

Chapter 18

The next day, everything was coming up roses for me. For the first time, Farmer and Gideon couldn't shut up and it wasn't just to ream me out. All I had to do was sit back during our recap meeting and watch the compliments roll in. But I knew that expectations were high for my sixth fight.

I reluctantly basked in the glow. Staying quiet when they released me even earlier without having watched the video playback. So I decided to see what was up with Mark. Yesterday, he had already excused me from rehearsal. But I'd much rather watch him dance. At least before I was due home.

I walk up the gym steps to see Mark coming out of Studio One.

And it took everything in me not to run to him.

To the world, we were still just associates. No more than amicable strangers.

He's leaning down on the floor, gathering his things into a bag. Completely unaware that I had even come in. Concentrating on collecting his things. The room was empty. "Hey, stranger."

He picked up his bag and spun around. His stance instantly relaxed and he came over and gave me a hug. Kissing me quickly on my forehead.

A moment that's so sweet it's like salve to my wounded heart.

"I wasn't expecting you today. I'm actually about to leave," Mark said, walking me back towards the door. "Since we didn't have a class or date I thought I'd go visit an old student of mine. She's in a nursing home." He stopped and held my hand. "She doesn't get as many visitors as she used to."

"Man, that's really sweet of you," I said. "Do you think she would mind another visitor?"

"You want to come?"

"Yeah, why not," I nodded.

He looked pleasantly surprised and agreed. But more than anything I was glad to be getting out of this building. Just being together put us in the dangerous orbit of being found out. And the cab ride over gave us some time to talk. Without the prying ears of my aunt and son.

The driver seemed to sense enough not to talk our ear off. As we cruised through the city to the suburbs. Like we were in a world to ourselves. A small box of cookies sitting on his lap, wrapped with twine. I was starting to realize that this was just Mark. He was always this thoughtful with people he cared about. Now I was one of those people. "When I came in earlier, the only thing I could think about was how damn perfect you looked, it's sickening."

He laughed. "Come on, I'm not perfect."

"Says only perfect people."

"If I'm perfect why do I always think of great comebacks to slights four hours too late."

I laughed. "Try again."

"I've never read War and Peace, but am not above claiming I did at snotty parties. When in fact, I've only read the Wiki page."

I was actually impressed. "I cannot believe you. You actually read the Wiki page. I've never even bothered. Once people hear that I'm a boxer, they don't expect much up here," I replied honestly, tapping the side of my head.

He turned and looked out the window as if he were thinking for a moment. Turning back to me excitedly he said, "I used to have a roommate that was borderline OCD, but it took a scary turn to the point where he was like policing me. He would come into my room, and going through my things, just to clean. Throwing my stuff away. So I got back at him."

"How so?"

"I mixed his shampoo with Nair. Would a perfect guy do that?"

"That's pretty terrible." I was just glad that he was equal parts mischievous and sweet. It appeared as if he could tame my bad side and keep up with my good side.

"Okay then, I'm not perfect. But what about you, Miss badass, tell me something about you?"

"Something definitely not badass would be...that I tuck myself in under the covers at night very tightly. So things can't get me. I might have a slight fear of the dark."

"Slight?"

"I sleep with a flashlight on under my pillow. A huge one, just in case it needs to double as a weapon. And my aunt instantly knew something was up the night you came over. Because the hallway light wasn't on. She mentioned it a couple of days later when she was teasing me about you."

"How have you been, since, you know?" His voice trailed off at the end as if he didn't mean to bring up this tough subject. But needed to ask.

"I take the train by myself sometimes really late. Lately, I notice everything and everyone. I nearly gave myself a heart attack one day because I thought someone was following me home. It turned out to be one of my neighbors. I almost kicked the shit out of her."

"Really?"

I nodded because I'm too ashamed to admit that I'm a chicken shit. The robbery certainly hasn't helped with my fear of the dark either.

"You're the strongest person I know. I don't think anything you've told me makes you any less so. You're like this really spry cat. All cute and adorable and unassuming. But if I were to back you into a corner, you'd claw the heck out of my eyes. You're dangerous, even when you think you're not. There is nothing in this world that you have to be scared of. The world should be scared of you."

"Thanks."

He grabbed my hand and brought it to his lips. Kissing my knuckles. "But whenever you are scared, you can always call me. I'll always be there for you. I slay dragons, crackheads, and annoying 10-year-olds with ice cream dreams."

My brow furrowed at that last one.

"I'll explain that last one some other time."

"Hello, guys we're here," the cab driver stated, having remained quiet for most of the ride. "Thanks for using, DRIVE."

Honestly, I had never been to a nursing home before. From the outside, the place looked more like a hotel than a nursing home. The gated garden path traveled around the side indicating that it was much more than that. Like they were hiding a heavenly oasis from the world.

He grabbed my hand and led me inside. Bringing a smile to my face and a blush to my cheeks. Not because I don't like PDA, but because

I'm not used to it. Even Owen is at the stage where he thinks holding my hand in public makes him look like a wuss. Although, he still manages to surprise me sometimes. But being with Mark kind of feels like bouncing on clouds of cotton candy. No matter where we were.

Once inside, I was instantly surprised by how state-of-the-art the place looked. My limited experience with nursing homes would have me believe it was more like an insane asylum than a place that I could actually see myself retiring in. In the place of grey and faded walls. Was a bright cream and maroon color. The receptionist and nurses were welcoming and friendly. Instead of the sour faces that you would expect from people who had been working long hours with little respect. A small waiting area off to the side that would resemble the living room of anyone's favorite granny. Flashing our IDs in order to get two visitor passes.

I watched as Mark charmed everyone who approached. Yet, I was no afterthought because he made me feel incorporated in everything. Introducing me as his girlfriend for the first time. Rendering me speechless but in a good way. I guess I wasn't going to regret coming after all. A few of the nurses even seemed to be slightly envious at the sight of him with another woman.

"You already know her room number. Just head on back." The nurse's voice was syrupy sweet as she handed us the sticky badges to put on our chests. Her eyes never left Marks. But jealousy was never my jam.

"Actually, it's a nice day out. Can we sit in the garden?" He asked her breezily. Appearing completely oblivious to her stark struck wonder.

"Of course, please wait here."

Ten minutes later, she reappeared with a sweet woman in a wheel-chair. A small, navy blue gradient wool shawl was thrown over her shoulders. White orthopedic shoes on that didn't have a speck of dirt on them. It made me wonder if she ever got up out of their chair. A blue and white peplum dress paired with a white blazer.

"She hasn't been doing that well today. But maybe that will change now that you're here." The nurse chimed in

She didn't appear to be aware of our presence.

"Sherry, this is Mr. Wade, your former dance teacher, and dear friend. He's come to spend some time with you."

"Who?" she mumbled, looking out of sorts as she grabbed the nurse's hand. She looked at us wryly as if we came to steal her purse.

The nurse pats her hand gently. "Don't worry they just want to spend time with you. You will be in good hands."

Mark looked over at me gingerly. "She has dementia."

I took his hand, wishing that was good enough to transfer my strength to him. "It's okay."

Looking up at the nurse, I nodded for her to take the lead. She wheeled Sherry back out the way we had come. And I felt like we were following behind her like a helpless funeral procession. Our expressions somber. She stopped in front of the gate and pulled a pair of keys out of the pocket of her scrubs. Revealing the oasis-like some sort of magic city.

"You guys got it from here?" She pointed, holding open the gate for us.

Mark handed me the box of cookies. Chocolate chip was written on the sides of the box in cursive. Stepping up to the chair like a batter out on the green. However, the view left me breathless. It was like the garden of Eden with sculptures and rose beds and wildflowers. There was even a small fountain with a cherub spitting water. Small loveseat-sized benches were scattered around the outside of the property near the path.

"I'll leave you guys alone. But no dancing with her Mark," the nurse chided.

I wondered what that was about, but didn't ask too painfully aware that I was the stranger in this equation. She closed the door behind us without locking it. He pointed to her room and the lovely view of the garden that she had on the first floor.

Mark's eyes looked clouded as if he wanted to cry, and it reminded me of what a good man he was. Choosing a bench that was in the middle of the path. And far enough away from the buildings prying windows. I briefly wondered if that was on purpose.

Sherry was talking as if she were giving us a tour. I enjoyed it, but I wondered if it was just breaking Mark's heart that she couldn't remember that it wasn't his first time. He pulled the wheelchair up to the bench where we were sitting.

"Sherry, this is my girlfriend, Michelle. She's actually a boxer."

"Ohh, I always did love a girl who was the master of her own destiny," she grinned broadly, briefly glancing down at the sweets in my lap. "Are those for me?"

"Yeah, I thought we all could share." He pulled out some napkins from the inside of his breast pocket. Pulling out two cookies from the box, I handed them to her. I took one and nibbled. It wasn't really my cheat day.

"I'm sorry that I can't get out here as often as I used to, Sherry. But you look beautiful. Not a hair out of place. So I know they're treating you right."

"That's sweet of you to say, young man."

A cursory answer hit him right in the chest and caused him to sniffle a bit. Seeing him this torn up made me want to reach out and grab him. But I kept my hands folded around that box.

"I still remember that song you like," he said, pulling his phone out of his pocket and turning it up, placing it gingerly on the arm of the wooden bench.

The music slowly played and it was like she came to life. "Mark?"

He turned away from her and wiped the stray tear from his face. Appearing to turn back to her as if he were unfazed. When he was barely holding it together. Who was this woman to him?"

"How long has it been?" Sherry asked, reaching out slowly to grasp his hand.

For a second she looked around as if she were confused about her whereabouts. Her gaze landing on me still sitting on the bench. "I'm just a friend of Mark's," I said, waving awkwardly.

"Are you taking his dance class like I was? Take my word for it, young lady, you're in great hands."

He barely nodded his head, standing to his feet. Not even bothering to relinquish her hand. It became painfully obvious what the nurse meant when she said not to dance with Sherry. She gingerly kicked her legs rests to the side and got to her feet with his help. Her muscles creaked.

My gaze flew down the path and I wondered if it was supposed to be up to me to talk him out of this. But when I looked back at them, I knew it wasn't.

"Can I have this last dance?" he asked his voice tight and controlled.

"With you, it's never the last one," she said, her voice breaking from misuse.

I don't know why, but I'm glad that they got to share this moment together. He wasn't moving fast or even going very far. It was the slowest 2-step I'd ever seen and it had to be a world record. Yet, there was no question that this dance was above reward. The shifting afternoon sun drifting over the bushes lit them up as if they were visiting angels. For a moment, I could see myself falling completely in love with this man who knew that no student should be forgotten. I'd never see Darren or my dad crying over me, least of all their own mothers.

"Such a beautiful song. Did I ever tell you the story of how my father came to write it?" She looked at me fleetingly, but I know that its Mark to whom she is really asking.

"I don't think we have the time to hear that story. I just found myself thinking about you and I had to stop by. If anything, it's nice to know that you haven't forgotten anything I taught you."

She huffed, and sat down, breathing heavily. "Such a flatterer you are. But there are lots of things that I am forgetting."

He leaned against the side table. "The important things you never forget."

"You danced beautifully," I said quietly, chest knotting up with my own unspent tears. "Hopefully, this one can get me to look half as graceful."

He looked back at his phone as the music stopped. Picking it up and looking at it with slumped shoulders as if it held all his hope.

"You will always be my favorite dancer," he said, pocketing his phone before leaning over and grabbing the woman's hand. But she was already gone.

"Oh, am I doing another garden tour again? You have to excuse me sometimes I can get a little spacey."

He nodded. "Yeah, you were telling us about your favorite flower."

"I love wildflowers. We should all be so free."

I blinked back my tears. "So true." I leaned over and whispered, "She's lucky to have you."

"Most of her family has already passed on, but she has lived a full and memorable life. It's just a shame that she can't remember it." He pointed to Sherry's hand. "Please, eat your cookies."

She looked down into her hand as if she forgot she was holding them. Finishing them off with the fervor of a delighted child. Who knew their mother never let them have any. Her knowledge of gardening was impressive. Somewhere mid-talk, Sherry had fallen asleep. A crumpled napkin in her hand. Crumbs on the corner of her mouth. He gingerly took the napkin out of her hand and wiped the crumbs from her mouth. She took a haggard breath but did not awaken.

"To know that you haven't forgotten her must be its own peace. At least it would be for me," I said after a while.

He smiled bashfully. "I guess."

I looked up at the sky. The sun beaming down on my cheeks put a blush on my cheeks, before I gathered the courage to stare into his eyes. "This is a wonderful thing, Mark Wade."

He reached over and grabbed a cookie from the box. The dozen slowly disappeared. He turned to face me with such a warm smile on his face, that I instantly wanted to know everything about him. "So outside of dance. What started this devotion to older people. I know you run the senior's dance class too, right?"

"I do. Actually, I started it, and it was one of the best decisions I've ever made. I just could use the break right now with the contest and all." He rubbed my index finger with his thumb, and it was the most intimate thing I've ever felt. Not even looking at me as he recounted his tale. "My parents, love them, but they were like extra new age. One of those let the child decide what they want to be kind of people. Which came in handy when I wanted to dance."

"To impress that girl." I snickered, squeezing his hand knowingly.

"Yes, but they didn't know that. I just appreciated them not giving me a hard time about it. Dance is for girls type crap. I got that from my grandfather."

I suppose that would make my own father enlightened as well. He certainly wasn't conforming to gender norms. Despite what I wanted. However, if that new ageism was responsible for Mark then it must be some good. I think I'm going old school with Owen and he was turning out fine.

"But I also had a grandfather in my life, who was pretty influential. I worshiped him. He was responsible for teaching me how to change a tire. We used to rough house in the backyard when mom wasn't looking. That's how I learned how to fight. My most memorable times were playing football with him and dad out at the park. The only time my father would acknowledge traditional gender sports. It's kind of funny looking back on it now."

"Sounds awesome actually."

"I didn't appreciate any of it then, but I do now."

"Perspective is everything," I replied, wishing that my view of my father was different.

"I didn't know it then, but my grandfather had a gambling problem. He made some bad decisions and allowed it to pull him down. Losing money left and right. Until he owed more than he could pay back to some loan sharks. He got desperate and decided to rob the neighbors. When he knew they would be out of the house. Sell their stuff and recoup whatever is left. One neighbor came home early. Despite them being friends for years, a fight ensued. That neighbor died and my grandfather went to jail for life."

My eyes nearly popped out of my head. "Oh my God."

"At that moment, he certainly wasn't innocent, but his impact on my life was. Everything he gave me was good and made me who I am. Because of him and my grandmother, I know how important grandparents are. And I'm not going to forget him or any senior that impacts my life positively. No one deserves to be left behind."

"Is he still—?" I hedged.

"Yeah, I go see him once a month."

I looked at Sherry, who was still sleeping. "I think we should get her back inside before she prunes. Maybe we can sneak these cookies into her room."

He smiled mischievously, "I'm totally down. You know they wont let her have them."

I shrugged my right shoulder, sneakily. "You know I got you."

Chapter 19

Waiting until Tuesday morning to see Mark again was almost torture. It was our first dress rehearsal. Of course, my closet being limited I had to buy a dress for the occasion. Settling on a simple purple midi dress that my auntie helped me pick out. Still walking on air from my visit with his senior friend where we had lunch after. The calls of motherhood drew me back home soon after. We still have been texting and sexting back and forth in his absence. But it only made me crave his touch more.

The way he bared his soul to me about holding older people in high regard was enough to have me wanting to jump his bones again. It's as if he peels back another layer and there's just more soft putty underneath. I can sometimes be a little harsher than him; I get that. But every time my natural instinct to lead kicks in, he quickly shows me who's boss out on that dance floor. He exudes controlled strength that he parcels out like a lion aware of the boundaries of his kingdom.

And maybe it's just the fact that he always treats me like a lady in every situation that's so endearing. In a way that makes me less afraid to be girly and allow him to lead. Chivalry isn't dead. And I love when he opens doors for me. Or simply takes my hand and leads the way. He really is the truth.

Over the weekend, I got word of the guys wanting to blow off a little steam tonight. That usually means some hard drinking. The person with the nearest bout was automatically designated, the driver. That meant me. So I found myself texting my auntie Shannon furiously in the hopes that she could babysit tonight. In my Mark-fueled haze, I'd failed to warn her earlier.

But it wasn't looking good for me.

She had some sort of corporate event tonight, and I would need to find a new babysitter. I had gotten to rehearsal a little early so that I could have time before dance practice to make some calls. The receptionist had given me a fake smile that said, she wished the phrase, break a leg, was a real thing.

"I'm hurt," Mark's teasing voice instantly lifted my mood and my gaze from my phone.

But I still couldn't recall what he said, "What?"

"I've been here 15 minutes now and you still haven't noticed," Mark laughed, coming to sit beside me wearing a muted pink shirt and ripped jeans.

I ran my hands down the front of his shirt. Sculpting out his muscles with my fingertips. Kissing him openly and deeply. His tongue created a waterfall of tingles in my secret place. Pulling away from him breathlessly, I said, "I noticed."

He searched my face, his desire evident.

Sending little girl me shrieking into the morning. My heart wanted to stop. I even had to resist the urge to look around and make sure that I was the one deserving of all this gorgeous. "We really need more alone time."

"Yeah," he said slowly taking my phone from my hand. "But now that I have earned your attention back. Tell me who stole it?"

"Owen," I said apologetically, snatching the phone back. My gaze went to the door when I thought I saw a shadow pass over the small window. Before squinting down at my phone again.

His finger trailed along my jawbone and he drew my attention back to him. "What's the matter with Owen? Is he still getting bullied?"

"No, nothing like that." Dropping my hands in my lap in pseudo defeat. "I'm supposed to go out with the guys tonight and Auntie Shannon can't babysit. So I'm trying to find a replacement. It's not as if this is super important, but when you're a girl in a male-dominated industry. Any little thing can be perceived as I don't belong."

His brow furrows and he nods as if contemplating what I have said, "I'll watch him for you."

That was unexpected.

"You don't even have to pay me. This first one will be free of charge. Although, I can't promise you how much I'll charge the next time."

My thoughts immediately splinter into a thousand different directions. I hope he didn't think I was fishing for help. Owen was my kid to parent and I certainly wasn't trying to shake that the first chance I got with my new boyfriend. Besides I could already hear my auntie Shannon in my head complaining.

Yet, he was sweet for even offering. It was more than Darren would ever have done. Dad was not the babysitting type either. And we still weren't on speaking terms after that whole episode with Darren in the gym. My only hope was that he wasn't using our fight as an excuse to be on another binger.

"You don't have to babysit Owen just because we're dating," I told him, with a firm motherly tone.

"Can I babysit because someone I care about needs to go to a career event?" he asked me with one eyebrow raised. "Plus, the kid is like extra cool."

I'm speechless. No one ever thinks about me or Owen except my auntie Shannon. I grab his hand and blink back the tears threatening to turn me into a baby. He placed his hand on top of mine.

"I understand perfectly what you mean. Some careers just come with their own social politics. When I first started here, I felt like I had to go to everything, in order to be accepted. And to a certain extent you do because no one knows you well enough to perceive it as anything else." He lifts my hands to his lips and kisses them gingerly. "I can only imagine how it is for you being a woman and one of the gym's main stars."

"Okay, then I accept your offer. After I talk to Owen and make sure it's okay."

"I'm good with that," he said, getting to his feet and reaching back to me. "You ready to dance?"

I did my best James Brown impersonation. "I'm twinkle toes."

"Of course, if you'd like to continue to panic to burn calories then I get it?"

I scrunched my nose up and laughed. "Since when does that work?"

"Since...now."

I looked around and kicked one of my gym shoes towards him.

He ran out of reach, laughing heartily. "Come on, when you're stressed you get this little vein in your neck like you've been working out for hours."

I looked at him aghast. "No, I don't."

He took me in his arms and nuzzled my neck. "I'll kiss it and point it out for you."

"You better stop. Before someone walks in." My smiling reflection stared back at me. Even as I betrayed my words and lifted my neck for easier reach. His soft lips were lightly pressed against the vein in my neck.

"Fine, we do have to work," he said, pulling away from me. "Dancing is just a conversation between two people. So talk to me."

"It is cheaper than therapy."

He went over to the radio and put on Tina Turner's The Best. I hollered, recognizing the feel-good music and driving beat.

He laughed. "Oh, you know this one."

Almost forgetting that we were supposed to be practicing I started to sing to him. He started blushing profusely and maybe I was talking to him personally. Putting on a show like I did that first night. Dancing around him seductively and wildly. Letting the dance lead me. This time I hadn't completely forgotten what he taught me. Throwing in some recognizable moves that left him drooling.

He fell to his knees and began to crawl after me as I pretended to reel him in. My hips and shoulders bopped along to the music. He leaned back on his legs and gestured for me to come to him. Propping one leg up as if he might propose. I skipped to him still singing along and sat on his knee. Throwing my hands around him as the song ended. "You are pretty cool."

I stood up when the song automatically replayed, and we stared into each other's eyes.

"You see how you were just now. Don't be so focused on the steps that you forget to dance."

This time we danced a lot slower and went through the steps of the dance.

He ended up clapping when we finished. "Just like that. Dancing should look easy. To the audience, they know you're doing something physically demanding and hard. But by the end, you've got to look like it was just a walk in the park. And you know you've succeeded when you get an encore."

He took off his shirt as he was already beginning to sweat. My eyes lit with hunger as I trailed the cut of his abs with my gaze. But there would be plenty of time for fun later. Over two hours of practice time flew by quicker than I wanted it to. Saddened, when I knew it was time for me to leave him and return to my double life as a boxer. But I knew time was against me during these brief transition periods. Which is why I flew out of rehearsal to get downstairs. Only to run smack dab into Farmer.

Taking a step back from him, I plaster on my best everything is fine smile. "Hey, you're here early."

Without giving me an answer, he turns on his heel and heads downstairs to the gym. I looked back at the closed door of Mark's studio hesitantly. The receptionist cleared her throat obnoxiously drawing my gaze. Only to find her nursing a satisfied smile. Standing to my full height, my heart started to pound as I made my way down the stairs. Maybe that shadow wasn't just my imagination. Hoisting my gym bag higher on my shoulder, I said stay cool.

I got downstairs to find the gym half empty. Only a couple of amateurs huddled in the corner using the punching bag. The receptionist ducked her head down to her paperwork as if she too knew a storm was brewing. Why did we even have a receptionist? It was just a clipboard with a pen attached. What else was there to it?

"So how long have you been here?" I asked Farmer hesitantly.

"You looked good up there."

"Let me explain," I said, my stomach-churning.

He shook his head. "It's pretty self-explanatory. That's where you are when you're not in the gym with me." I looked down, well maybe it was simple. "But if you want to win Nunn, an actual championship. You're going to have to stop the prima ballerina shit and get serious. A lot of money is on the line. So if you're even late to the next practice, I'm dropping you."

"Come on," I pleaded. "I thought you of all people would understand."

"Understand what, you think I care that you're licking down some guy. You're a grown woman. What I do care about is you lying to me when you say you're committed to getting this championship. And then you're splitting your time between this and hardwood floors. At the worst possible time."

"You know I feel about boxing."

"Yeah I do," he nodded, still incensed. "Just like I know how many times I begged you to quit and you didn't. Or the times I asked you to stop and you wouldn't. Now you're on the plane of no return. Expecting the whole thing to turn around and about-face. It ain't gonna happen."

"That's not what I want."

He flexed his fingers as if he were going to strangle me. Clearly holding back his true emotions. "I saw you, it's only a matter of time. I know you're happy. But this ain't the business for happy. You're not on the road that veers off to somewhere else. This journey is headed straight to the ring and only the ring. And if you think you're going to disembark. You will ruin everything that Keith and I have worked for. But you don't even get to give a shit about that. Look at me and ask me if I really think Gideon will let you go without a fight?"

I swallowed the lump in my throat, throwing my gym bag out of the way. "I know my priorities. Get me in the ring."

He laughed, nodding at my jean booty shorts. "You may want to change first."

I over-corrected during practice to make up for the fact that I had been majorly reamed out. The bottom had fallen out from under me and I could no longer pretend that I could do both. So with every punch I threw, it felt like I had to prove that I really was second to none. That I fought for my spot and wanted to keep it. More importantly, I didn't want to make waves with Gideon. I loved my family too much to put them in danger.

Which only made me angry at the prospect of losing Mark. But thanks to our little audience, my presence at tonight's gathering just became mandatory. I had to squelch any rumors about my commitment before they started. Stopping any chance of it getting back to Gideon or my dad.

I also felt shitty for still asking Mark to babysit knowing that I was going to have to quit dancing. Breaking up with him however never crossed my mind. Either we would have to start meeting outside the gym/studio or I should finally come clean about my new relationship. But I had to talk to him first before making a decision like that. This mandatory social outing is making it impossible to find the time to do that. So it looks like will have to talk afterward.

"Hey, stink bug," Farmer said, entering my apartment and giving me a hug. Kissing my temple before giving Owen a handshake. The boy came flying out of his room like his pants were on fire. His Gameboy was abandoned on the floor.

"You're not going to be dancing tonight are you?" He asked as if that was the worse thing in the world.

I'm expecting him to launch into a full dance to prove that he really does have skills. After all, he was a man that took pride in his work. Instead, he said, "Great dancers are not great because of their technique. They are great because of their passion."

Owen didn't look convinced. "Says people who can't dance. Please tell me you cook okay?"

"I don't think you'd want anything I cook. I'm a pretty healthy guy. So will order pizza."

I shook my head. "He already ate."

Owen went back to his room with his head slumped as if he knew he almost had pizza. I led Mark into the kitchen to show him where I kept all Owen's emergency contact info. "Oh, I'm going to try not to stay late. I was hoping we could get some time together after the kid goes to sleep."

He twirled the small note in his hand with all Owen's info and likes and dislikes. "I'd like that."

Taking me into his arms, he kissed me with a passion that would ensure that I would be leaving early. Farmer was actually picking me up tonight. So I hurried downstairs to wait for him after saying goodbye to Owen. Glad when Farmer gave me the heads up that Darren and my dad would also be in attendance. I prepared for it to be a rough three hours. But I walked into a trap. A few jokes were made about the scene I had made. But Darren was able to turn it into some sort of girls are crazy bro code. With the help of my father calling me temperamental. Farmer's pleas for everyone to cool it fell on deaf ears. After two hours I was starting to feel like the odd man out. So I excused myself to the bathroom and just never returned. At least no one was talking about my commitment to boxing.

It was also 10 o'clock that had to be a sufficient enough time to have stayed out. Just so it doesn't look like I rushed back to be with Mark. Even though he was never far from my mind the whole time. My check-in call quickly revealed that I was annoyingly interrupting Owen's game time with Mark. There were only so many heavy sighing and eye-rolling to my questions that I could take. But it was good to see him happy and contented.

So I expected to come home to couch forts and potato chip crumbs on the carpet with loud music playing in the background. Some game on holding their attention to the point that they don't even hear me come in. The lampshade was crooked on the table with no reasonable explanation as to why. What I got instead was a basketball game on the living room TV. And my two favorite people were asleep on the couch. Mark's head rolled back on the couch, snoring lightly. My son was on the other end of the couch, his hands tucked underneath his head as drool fell from the corner of his mouth.

I took off my jacket and threw my keys on the table. Scooping Owen into my arms and carrying him into his room. His eyes fluttered open as soon as his head hit the pillow. He must have a sixth sense when it's bedtime? I rolled the cover on top of him and grinned. "Hey babe, how was tonight?"

"You weren't gone long enough. I almost convinced him to let me watch a scary movie," he groaned, his voice full of sleep.

I shook my head from side to side and kissed the side of his cheek. "I'll remember that next time."

"So he's going to babysit again?"

"Will see how things work out, but I think Auntie Shannon missed you today."

"I missed her too," he said groggily, his eyes heavy.

I cut the batman light on his side table off and slowly closed the door. Careful, not to wake him again. Only to squelch a laugh at the sight of Mark still knocked out. I came and sat beside him. Rubbing his leg, gingerly to wake him. He bolted up, looking around for Owen.

"It's all right, I took him to his room."

He rubbed his hands over his face and groan. "I don't think you realize how energetic you're not. Until you spend time with a kid."

I laughed. "You did great from what I heard."

He turned to me and exhaled loudly. "Good. I want my report card spotless."

I smirked. "You know you snore, right?"

"So I've been told. Is it obnoxious? Are you worried about losing sleep?"

I know I was supposed to tell him about Farmer and quitting dance. And we still needed to have a heavy conversation about whether to come out about our relationship or not, but I didn't want to do any of that. "I don't think I ever need to sleep again."

Those words might as well have been, open sesame because I was silenced with a kiss. An impulsive embrace that allowed our pent-up desire to take control. Instantly giving me a floaty feeling of being high above the sky. My skin was on fire as he lifted me into his arms and carried me back to my room. Our sloppy, hot kisses claimed each other's bodies as if we physically hungered for each other.

"We have to be quiet?" I whispered.

He smirked against my lips. "It's not me I'm worried about."

Tearing off each other's clothes like two wild teenage camp counselors trying to hide from the adults to get a quickie in. Instead of a sleeping little boy. His hand creeps underneath my shirt to brush across my pointy nips. Every kiss was a promise that he was only meant for me. I couldn't imagine having a connection this deep with Darren.

I closed my eyes and leaned back on the pillow knowing that I couldn't be in safer hands. Savoring the touch of his lips as he trailed kisses down my belly. Until he was tugging at the buttons of my jeans with his teeth and pulling them off. Tossing my panties to never-never land as his manhood drowned in the core of my being.

My fingernails trailed up and down his arms. The feel of his manhood filled me causing a rush as I lifted my hips to meet his. His hands tightened around my waist as his breathing quickened. My thighs shook as he plunged deeper and deeper into my mound making it harder to stifle my moans.

I can't even remember how many times I bit down on his shoulder to squelch the screams. My muscles spasmed as warm waves of pleasure crested over us.

He rolled over out of breath. Both of us stared up at the ceiling. "You think I can skip the gym tomorrow?"

I laughed. "Only if I can."

Chapter 20

Despite our growing relationship, I'm still not ready for a man to stay over with me and Owen. So when my alarm went off early that morning. I snuck him out the front door again. Just glad there wasn't a nosy auntie sleeping on the couch this time. He grabbed his shoes and jacket and waited until he was outside the door to throw them on. However, we made plans for him to escort me to tonight's fight. I almost snickered when he was more than on time, he was early.

"This is your sixth one. Only one away from the belt. That's got to be surreal. The only thing I keep going back to is how crazy your work ethic is balancing your classes with me and practicing for your fights. You really are a phenom."

"Thanks," I said, but in a way that communicated that I genuinely did appreciate his opinion. Still unable to tell him about Farmer's words and what that might mean for us. It wasn't that I was afraid to. I just wasn't sure I was ready to do anything about it. "I just can't wait until it's over and I can focus just on dance."

"I'm glad you let me take you."

He twirled the string of my sweat pants around his fingers and pulled me to him. French kissing me in a way that it felt like we were making love all over again. Leaving me breathless when he pulled away. I should be concerned about all this PDA in the parking lot of the arena. But frankly, I didn't give a damn.

Basking in the glow of Mark's praise, we cross the parking lot into the arena of what will be the fight of my life. The first fight that I've ever been nervous about. This qualification match wasn't with some girl who found herself in the wrong field after being told by the wrong trainer that she was the next great white hope. Just so that he could get into her pants. This was the best that the boxing world had to offer and she deserved the belt just as much as I did. But didn't go through the things that I had to get here though. And that was an edge that I intended to use against her. It was a layer of hardness that couldn't be taught in a gym.

"Hey, don't distract her with your lovey-dovey goo. My girl got to focus," Farmer said, coming up behind us and cutting through the middle. Breaking our grip, but only temporarily. It appeared as if we both had made it to the arena at the same time.

Mark turned to me shocked, a look of concern on his face.

But it was Farmer who answered first. "Yeah, you're little secrets out. Now stay back until the fight is over."

Shaking my head, I let out an exasperated sigh that's half love half frustration with the man. "Yeah, he found out about us yesterday. I've been meaning to talk to you about that."

He gave my hand a comforting squeeze. "We can talk about it tonight after your win."

"That would be great," I said, as we reluctantly released each other's hands.

"Good luck, stink bug." He continued down the hall to the audience seating as I was led in the opposite direction to my changing room. Trying to get my mind off him and into the upcoming fight.

"Don't you think you two played it a little close coming in here locked hand and hand?" Farmer asked me, once we were alone.

"Probably, but if your lecture taught me anything. It was that Gideon equals bad and you can't deny happiness."

"Words to live by."

"Why do you work for him if you think he's so horrible?" I asked doubtfully. Unable to comprehend how a good guy like Farmer could become tied to someone like Gideon.

"Somebody has to protect the sheep from the wolf."

And then it clicked as a bell had rung for the final round. That's why they call him Farmer. Instead of his real name Paul Fedora.

I barely had any time to mull over this epiphany, when we walk into the changing room to see Gideon and my dad waiting for me. Nodding hello to Gideon, I barely acknowledged my dad's presence. Plopping my gym bag with my change of clothes on the wooden bench. My anger...and hurt over my father's actions would fill this room to the ceiling. I could swim in the tears I wanted to spill but couldn't.

"Farmer, give us a minute. James and I have to talk to Michelle. Alone!" Gideon barked.

My gaze darted to the safety of the door begging him with my eyes for him to take me with him. Crossing my arms over my stomach, I kept deftly still as if the slightest movement would find me in the clutches of their claws and bared teeth. I was naive to think that my father would miss the biggest fight of my life. This was what he had been working for.

Farmer didn't speak another word. Backing out slowly, scratching his nose in concern. "I'll just be outside."

"Hey, daughter."

"James," I said, my upper lip curling in disgust. He's been ghosting me since the breakup. Only to ignore me in favor of the boys club when everyone went out to the bar. Now he wants to have a daughter when it's convenient. He must think I'm stupid. Or maybe just falling for his bullshit again.

"Don't be that way?" He grinned with all the charm of an alley possum. "You know I still love you."

When Gideon laughed, my gaze quickly flickered to him. "Is this about today's fight? It's my sixth fight. I'm ready for it. I don't need no pep talk."

"Do I look like the pep talk type?" he quipped, shaking my father's hand as if they were co-conspirators. My toes curled up in disgust in my gym shoes at the sight. "This is all business, Michelle. I just want you to go into this next fight, understanding how important it is for you to win. Because you're losing the championship."

It literally felt like chunks of the moon fell out of the sky to hit them over the head. There was no way that the words that had fallen out of their mouth were natural. Winning is all I do. They both need me to win for the real money to come rolling in. To do otherwise would be putting Owen's future at stake. A possible $450,000 down the drain when it's picked up by PPV. This is why they were airing this fight on basic cable to drum up anticipation. When it comes to business, I may move to the side to let others lead, but I wasn't stupid. There was a lot they would have to account for to make what they said make sense.

"Don't look dumb, you heard him." My dad's stern rebuke was enough to unthaw my frozen thoughts. Flipping him the bird in response. I might not be able to do that to Gideon, but my dad could get the business. Like an annoying little parrot that sits on Gideon's shoulder.

"Someone wants to explain to me why I'm losing Fight Seven, The Championship bout that will air on PPV?" Looking between them both, when the only person I wanted to hear from was Gideon. But all I got was silence. "Don't all speak up at once. I'm just the fighter in the ring. What do I need to know?"

"We've struck up a once-in-a-lifetime deal. Everything is on the line here. But this has the potential to make us millions far more than we would get just from sales."

I stared at them stunned. The money we were making before wasn't chump change.

"We all get a healthy piece of the pie and you get to quit like you always wanted."

My head flinched back slightly, not even able to enjoy the possibility of being free. It was just a carrot they were dangling in front of me to entice me. They had no intention of ever giving me my freedom. Even if I won the championship, there were still endorsement deals and holding on to the belt as more and more people came straight for the newbie's head. What were they really trying to pull here?"

Gideon walked up to me and placed a firm hand on my shoulder. "I still got Brooke with some well-placed promo. I can bill her as your little sister and have her in your place in a blink of an eye." I swallowed hard as I stared into his cold eyes. "But I want to be sitting on a mountain first. And you're going to do that for me."

Looking around him at my dad, who was just sitting back rubbing his hands together like some Disney villain. A weird smile on his face indicated another one of his front teeth had fallen out. He was clearly on board with anything that came out of this wolf's mouth.

"What if I don't?" I asked hesitantly, not sure how far I was willing to take this newfound voice of mine. Just knowing that my dad doesn't speak for me anymore? I'm the master of my own destiny. And when I step into that ring, I want to win or lose on my own merit. It's all I've worked for. That one moment of greatness.

"I'm sorry, I've given you too much freedom here," he said, his grip tightening on my shoulder.

"Dad," I said sounding a little breathy to my own ears. I wanted to yelp out in pain but held it in. Biting the inside of my cheek so hard I'm sure I'll draw blood.

"I've somehow led you to believe that you have choices here and that's my mistake. I tend to spoil my girls. It's a weakness. We all have weaknesses."

My heartbeat thrashed in my ear as I immediately thought of Owen. The hostility in his voice created its own drumline in my body.

"My partner happens to love his grandson. But helpfully, he's not the only one that you hold dear. There's a cunt of an aunt too. I watched you two together for a few days, just to make sure that he wasn't lying to me. But you love her don't you."

"Yes."

"Keep her safe then." He nodded. "I can't wait until you win this fight tonight." He grabbed my chin and shook it back and forth. "My girls are always reliable."

He left me speechless, staring at my dad for some sort of help and compassion. My intention rested solely on him, even as Keith and Farmer were allowed back into the room. My gaze made him squirm like the worm I knew that he always was. Trying to work out in my mind why I haven't committed homicide yet.

"What happens if I don't win tonight?"

Sensing some tension the guys stay silent as they come to stand between us. As if at any moment they may have to play referee to another bout backstage. His gaze fluttered between the pair like they were my bodyguards. Wringing his hands like a crackhead strung out unmentionable substances. But he need not worry about their actions. Just mine.

"This is our moment. You're going to win. That's it."

He sprang out of there as if his pants were on fire. Only stopping long enough to kiss me on my cheek. I couldn't remember the last time he kissed me. Whatever Gideon promised, it must be bad. Wiping my cheek with the back of my hand, I collapsed on the bench next to my bag. A headache coming on fast and furious.

"What was all that about? What did Gideon want?"

I just shook my head. Unable to form the words. How many times had he warned me about this day? It's hear and I don't know what to do.

Farmer got to his knees in front of me. "Speak to me, kid?"

I looked up into his eyes. My vision was blurry as tears cascaded down my cheek. He took me into his arms and crushed me to him. And all I could do was cry into his shoulder. Keith's gentle, but strong hands rubbed my back in support.

I got ready in silence after that. No one needed the details to know that a change had taken place. My headphones were on my head, the whole time as if they were my visible lifeline. But my normal song just didn't do it for me. Especially when there was a literal life on the line. Skipping through my playlist, I stumbled upon True by Amaranthe. Running through it once, I quickly showed it to Keith.

"I want this playing on the loudspeakers."

Keith left to talk to the sound guy and I replayed the song over and over. Adjusting the wide headphones over my ear as I nodded along. This was the fire I needed.

Farmer stood behind me and placed the robe on my shoulder. It felt like I was Batman being fitted for my cape. My audience was just innocent civilians who needed to be saved from another boring show. Dancing in place as I followed my team out to the arena. But when I stepped inside, it was like a different feeling had completely overtaken me. This wasn't the Local 399. This was bigger.

I was at the bottom of a vacuum being stared at by giants. There screams for more, and more were reminiscent of those from the audiences of the Colosseum screaming for blood. So loud that it drowned out the music piping in from my headphones. And that alone made me more scared of them than what awaited me in the ring. The preliminary fight was long over. I almost wanted to stand in the middle of the runway and scream to their faces, are you not entertained?

Springing to the ring like a Leopard, and putting on a show. Binding the top rope down as I did a little dance. It was out of character for me, but I needed it to be. To strike some sort of suspicion in the minds of those who follow me religiously when I lose my seventh fight. Maybe they will blame it on me being too overconfident going into the sixth one.

But it wasn't hard to notice that Yuki was out of shape. Not to mention I was coming off a 5-0 lead. While Yuki Vieil was entering on a 4-1 run. That left me feeling confident as I hopped around and listened to the announcer running off our stats. Saluting Amber 'Shatterproof' Spence who sat ringside. She'll be happy she's keeping her title.

The bell rang. Yuki executed a few jabs to my midsection obviously trying to figure me out. But I let her know quick with some straights to the head that I was serious. If she was going to win this she would have to stop thinking like a B player and bring her A-game. As if she heard my thoughts she came out hot trying to hit me with the flurry and almost lost her balance. She paid for that when I made the next body shot hurt. By Round 2, Farmer even commented that my countering was perfection.

It became clear, by Round 4, that Vieil was a crude fighter with just the jab. I began to wonder if the seventh fight would be like this. Because there was no way I could reasonably lose a fight like this. Vieil was losing to herself. Letting her get in a few victory punches before I crashed down on her with all the force of a steel mousetrap. I hit her with a flurry of shots to the head that would send her mouthpiece flying. The referee quickly broke us up and sent everyone to their neutral corners until another was retrieved for her. I could only smirk at how easy this was. Getting in a few more shots before the bell rang. But this wasn't intended to be a long break as the bell for the fifth round sounded immediately.

Vieil got off a shot to my nose and I immediately thought it was broken. Stepping back to clear out my nostrils if it was bleeding. Her punches wild out of frustration. Backing me into a corner. It wasn't that Yuki was a bad fighter because it had obviously been working for her, but now she was out of her element. I battled out of the corner like an out-of-controlled boar, to pin Vieil against the ropes. Stealing an uppercut as we somehow reversed positions.

Admittedly, I played up the fight for the crowd. Staying on the inside allowed, Vieil sometime to fight back. This was my longest fight yet with 12 rounds, but it would also net me close to $90,000. So it would behoove me to drag this one out for as long as possible. Even if I was confident that I could lay her out. However, taking a beating may play to the crowd, but too many wrong hits can sometimes tire you out. So I had to balance that with conserving my energy. When the bell for the end of the 11th round rang, I was tired.

"You got to finish this fight. It looks like you're running out of gas out there," Farmer said, wiping the sweat from my forehead with a towel. My cheeks were practically hot to the touch and I knew I was turning red.

Keith shook his head. "You need to hit the gym harder."

I rolled my eyes. Between my dance classes and practice, I felt like that was all I was doing. But I agreed with Farmer that this needed to be finished.

Coming out when I needed this fight to end with my own uppercut and a right and left hook. Once I had her against the ropes, she tried to grapple with me to stop the onslaught. It gave her a reprieve, but like Mortal Kombat, all I heard in my head was, Finish Her.

And according to the unanimous decision I did.

Seventh Fight, here I come, ready to prove that Amber really is Shatterproof.

Chapter 21

After a month of rehearsal, which included me getting my stiff board shoulders to cooperate with the rest of my body. I was starting to feel like a pro that could rival Caliece. In another universe, maybe I would be the one to win $10,000 at the competition and a shiny new trophy. Farmer's voice was in my head, almost immediately, whispering not to be a sore winner. The only thing stopping me from sticking it to the prissy twig. Every time Caliece saw me she sidestepped out of my way as if I had some disease that was catching.

However, it was Darren coming out of Studio One that caught my eye. Had he been in there with Mark, alone? They're not even supposed to know each other, unless...

"What did you say to him?" I barked at Darren.

"Wouldn't you like to know?"

I must've been back in the ring because all I wanted was to wipe that smile off his face with my fist. Dropping my backpack by the reception desk in my haste. Just to follow him out into the parking lot as he tried to make a quick escape. Cracking my knuckles just in case I needed to grab him about the collar like the little weasel he was. I considered tripping him when he made it to the car. His eyes were overly bright as he looked back over his shoulder at me.

I don't wait for another invitation, grabbing the back of his shoulder and pulling him away from the open driver's side door. Whipping him around to face me. But the fear in his eyes quickly gave way to lust. As the hands that should be pushing me away wormed their way around my waist and pulled me close. It felt no better than being in a snake's grasp. Just as tight and twice as slimy.

"What the hell you doing!" I relaxed my grip on him, just enough to push his hands away. Stepping back when he tried it again. "I want to know what you said to him."

I'm aware of the fact that I'm shouting and in an upscale neighborhood such as this it would clearly be a scene. But I'd passed the point of caring. I would lay Darren out flat if I had to. My childish instinct was kicking in, and the little girl inside of me was highly upset. Daddy had shown up to take another toy, something I cared about and I couldn't let him get away with it. Except, exchange Daddy for Darren and not much had changed in my life.

"Nothing he shouldn't know."

Flashing him a cold smile, I thought about leaving him in front of our old studio as a tribute. A bloody mess that they would have to mop off the cement with a dirty mop head. Just being in his space was stifling. I laced my fingers together because surely I'd accidentally slap him.

With sadness tugging at the ends of my nerves, I looked back towards the building to pick up a clue as to what happened. I'm assuming that he had to see us together. Who was I kidding though, it was a miracle that he hadn't found out earlier.

"How did you find out?" I said, knowing that Darren wouldn't be forthcoming with the details, without a little prodding.

"I saw you with him at fight six."

Oh, so now the weasel speaks. With a huff, I crossed my arms over my chest. Did he see us at the same time as Farmer? Or had he seen us after, when we thought everyone had left? I guess it didn't matter now. "Darren, what are you going to do about it, huh? We're over. I don't owe you anything. And you never had any loyalty."

"Nothing," he smirked with a gleam in his eye. "Because when he knows you as I do. He ain't gone wont you. Some men like women who actually listen."

My back stiffened as I stood up straighter. His words sliced my heart open. But I wouldn't give him the time of day by showing it on my face.

"You don't know him."

"I know prissy boys like him, and so do you. Or have you been slumming it with me for too long?"

"Is that your problem? I'm elevating my game. You try doing the same. Or maybe you're used to playing with children on Blue Lagoon? Tell me, has she had her period yet?"

"You always did have a nasty bite. But you somebody else's problem now," he shrugged, turning to get into his car. As if he washed his hands of me instead of the other way around. Like I had caused him untold heartache. I kicked his front headlight as he pulled off. Flipping me the bird in response.

I sighed and looked back towards the dance studio. "Time for damage control."

Swinging the doors open, I'm surprised that there is no receptionist at the desk. A woman on a mission, I headed straight for Studio 1. Stopping, as I caught Caliece and Mark in an intense discussion with their heads together. He looked exhausted as if whatever he had endured had been mentally draining. Taking off his baseball cap to scratch the top of his head. But I never thought that Caliece would be his confidant. They didn't have a relationship like that. But now because of Darren they do. She looked like the type of woman that couldn't wait to be his shoulder to cry on. The type that didn't have problems like I did.

Raking my gaze over Caliece, I took her, I'm going to steal your man outfit in fully. She was wearing a white spaghetti strapped bodysuit. Some elegant blush-colored shorts were thrown on top. Did she always dance in such outfits? Or was this specifically for Mark's eyes only?

Jealousy. Annoyance. A blinding sadness. They all hit me directly below the diaphragm. The familiar feelings of inadequacy and just not being enough, threatening to bowl me over. Caliece's expression was sickeningly devoted as she casually touched his arm. A burning sensation hit the back of my throat and my mouth started to water. Suddenly, I wanted to vomit at the sight of them.

"Listen, ignore Edgardo. He just wants to break up a winning team to make it easier for him."

I hear his words, but the fact that he might not actually be talking about me hasn't computed yet. My thought, however, was cut short by his next statement.

"Now that I'm done with Michelle, I'll be more focused too."

"It's just nice to see you finally come to your senses." She danced around him like a pretty firefly. Doing a plie in front of him that almost resembled a bow. "She was never worth your time. It's just a pity that you had to learn that from her ex."

Without so much as a glance towards the door, he followed her with his eyes.

"I already knew who she was way before he showed up." Caliece looked up at him, the ultimate devoted subject. "She was never as beautiful or graceful as you. It was like she was playing at being a woman when you just are. Now I'm done allowing her to play with my emotions."

I'm awestruck. Mark was supposed to be smarter than this and he wasn't. He ate up everything Darren had said like some dope. It was hard even listening to this garbage. I stepped away from the door. Maybe I just never knew him. Taking a deep breath to calm the emotions that made me want to cry.

The movement must've caught his eye because he turned his startled blue eyes on me.

"Michelle, wait."

Darren's words replayed in my head as if he was standing right next to me, whispering in my ear, *I told you so.* Snatching my heart from my chest and crushing it in his hand. A personification of why I'd never had anything good. Because I was weak and easily manipulated. Even now all I wanted was for Mark to hold me in his arms and twirl me about the room. Or maybe I could just lay my head on his lap and we could laugh about what a big joke all this was. And I hated that I even wanted that instead of being strong enough to walk in and give him a piece of my mind.

But I knew that if we talked now, then I wouldn't be able to control my temper. I might even do more than just break his nose. My anger was like a candle burning down to its quick. When everything goes black it was going to get worse for everybody in the vicinity. But I wasn't protecting Mark, I was protecting myself. Clearing my throat, to shake off the pent-up rage, I replied, "We don't need to talk."

My hand was begging to knock the guilt off his face. But before I could react, I caught sight of my dad coming back up with the receptionist, out of the corner of my eye. Mark would never know that my dad just saved his life. A temporary band-aid on an open wound. For once, Darren had been right and I hated Mark for that.

Today, I didn't even have the option to run, I had to put some time in at the gym. Tomorrow, I'd have a stomach ache and put some distance between myself and this place. Owen would appreciate the extra time together. Although dodging questions like jabs to the head from my auntie wasn't going to be pleasant either.

Out of the corner of my eye, I saw my dad chatting up the receptionist. At this moment, I'd rather hear his nonsense than the lies and excuses Mark wanted to sell me.

Instead, I stepped into my dad's line of sight and picked up the bag I had thrown down earlier. He blinked as if he wasn't expecting to see me. Stepping away from the receptionist as if he had been caught with his hand in the cookie jar. My father always thought he was charming when really he was just skeevy. But I wasn't worried about that shriveled shlong.

"Hey, baby girl, just who I was looking for. I wanted to apologize."

I guess some men can surprise you. Looking back at Mark just as he came out into the hallway, and some men can't. "What is it, dad?"

He reminds me of every other man in my life, who was as fake as a three-dollar bill. Chasing the princess in the tower. And ignoring the women in the guard fighting beside him. He never had a clue as to how to deal with me, that's clear now. I just couldn't figure out, if I'm a loser for believing that he could or for opening my heart so easily. Knowing that I could fall in love with him. And once you've given someone you're heart you can't take it back.

There I go with that word, love. It wrapped itself around my hands and tied them. How have I managed to enter the ring with another wrong guy?

My dad led me by the elbow down the stairs to the gym. And I looked over my shoulder at Mark in a complete loss. Our gazes locked each other in a fight.

Chapter 22

"Hey Keith, let me spar with my daughter."

I rolled my eyes but nodded for him to hop out of the ring. As soon as we were safely downstairs, I threw myself into my training program to get my mind off Mark and my dad. Even if I was pressured into losing this fight, no one else was supposed to know that. So I had to proceed the same way that I would any other fight. Diet, train, repeat. But I wasn't going to feel guilty for leaving early.

It kind of felt like I didn't have the capacity to even process everything that I heard from Mark. I wanted to scream and lay my feelings at his feet. My heart was supposed to be safe with him. The fight had finally turned in my favor. I got the good guy. At least I thought I had. I told him all that yucky stuff about my father. There was no faking it, at least on my part, that I trusted him. Now he gets to watch me be eaten alive by his betrayal.

My dad pulled himself up on the ropes. Reaching back down for the pads from Keith, I immediately wished they had his face on them. Or Mark's or Darren's. Curse it. He only had two hands and my list was only growing. Maybe I should just tape a bunch of pictures to the punching bag. Of course, that wasn't sad at all. "You were looking really good out here. I needed a piece of the action."

"My girls working hard in there. What did you do to piss her off?" Keith laughed.

Taking a few swings at his left hand, I tried to tune them both out. A bull seeing red, his hand turned into a picture of Mark. Unable to stop remembering him with baby doh eyes filled with sorrow and guilt. But I only needed to conjure up images of Caliece dancing around him like an old-school music box to chase that way. Those same feelings of wanting to throw up returned.

"Your form is great too. Almost too perfect," he mumbled. Switching up his combos at the same time. I grunt an acknowledgment of his statement. Automatically aware that he was referring to my automatic loss. "And for some reason, it looks like you have actually gotten better. Like your movements are more languid."

"What the hell do you want dad? I'm trying to train here," I said, hitting him with a combination of hits and purposely missing the pads. Nothing that would actually hurt, just send a message.

He pounds the pads together as if to redraw my focus. I hid my face behind my gloved arms and do a little bobbing and weaving as I waited for my opening. There was no way I wasn't going to knock him on his feet. Accidentally of course. Throwing a couple of jabs at the pads to throw him off.

"This was the only way I knew that I could get close enough to you to tell you that you don't have to lose the fight?"

I hit him hard across the jaw. Sending him flat on his butt. Only to look down at him in disbelief. Holding up my gloved hand for Keith to stay out of it. "What did you say?"

He looked around ensuring that we weren't calling too much activity to the ring. "You heard what I said, little girl. You don't have to lose."

There's that word again. I wasn't sure, which L word I hated more, love or loss. They both held so much weight that it could feel like a tumor sitting on your heart or brain. The funny thing is I've heard the word lose said with more passion than the word love. I reluctantly helped him back to his feet and we resumed our sparring. Paying no attention to the fact that his little fall had heart his back.

"So what's this about? Or are you talking out of the side of your neck?" I mumbled, hiding my lips behind my gloves. Rubbing his back, insolently. He reluctantly puts up his pads and Keith falls back. Sensing that everything had fallen into normalcy.

"I went to Owen's school the other day, to take him out for Grandparents day. Which is conveniently once a week."

My eyebrows knitted together as I realized that my son had been keeping a secret from me. Positively amazed that I hadn't been notified by the school. Of course, he was on the pickup list. I hit his right hand. "So you've been taking Owen out of school once a week. For how long?"

"You're focused on the wrong details, baby girl. I usually go around recess. Give him some time to burn off some energy with his friends. Except when I got there, someone was already there."

Jab, duck, jab. Uppercut. Switch to your less dominant hand. Repeat. Jab, duck, jab. The rote memory of my training allowed me to focus even as my insides were spiraling. It was like he was bringing to life my very fears and I was helpless against it all. I don't even know if I was capable of hearing anymore, but this was Owen.

"Gideon…He didn't see me, but I saw enough to know that he wasn't keeping his promise. The boy swore that he just made a friend. No worse for wear, but it was clear that he was staking the place out. Insurance may be for if things go wrong."

Numbness set in as I realized that my fight with Gideon wouldn't be won with fists and gloves. My mind trying to do reps in order to figure out how to get out from under the spotlight. Anything that might help me save my family. But I was empty. It was like I had filled up Owen's cup with all the love and care that I could, but now mine was empty. And like the tin man and the scarecrow it left me without a heart or a brain to function. Every word was like a thousand pinpricks to the back of my neck and I couldn't even summon the strength to cry. "So how have things changed? Besides getting worse."

"He's gone back on his promise. I never wanted the kid hurt. So, you don't have to lose the fight because I plan on taking him down way before that."

The bright lights of the gym suddenly filled my eyes, confusing me so much that I didn't know whether to laugh or cry. I couldn't even feel grateful. All I could see was my dad being so drunk that he needed Darren to carry him out of the bar. I literally see him forcing me to stay with a man I hate so he can continue getting invites to after-parties. Throwing me under the bus in favor of the bro code. How was this man expected to do anything but disappoint me? Better still, how could I expect him not to make it worse?

"You still haven't learned that your old man always has something up his sleeve," he said, hitting back with the sparring pads. A visible sheen of sweat revealed that it was past time for him to relinquish the reins to Keith. I can even hear Keith from the floor asking if everything was all right and if he could still continue. "I got you into this business trust me to get you out."

"Why should I?" I asked, dropping my hands and facing him head-on. "You've been nothing but a disappointment to me. Now I'm supposed to trust you with my son's life. The life of my aunt. My only real family."

He shook his head, and slowly freed himself from the sparring pads. "You got a right to feel that way. I learned the hard way that all money ain't good money."

I followed suit and took off my gloves. Suddenly, I felt a little claustrophobic in this gym. As if the walls were closing in with 10-feet thick nail beds. "It's so sweet that Owen was able to bring you to your senses. Instead of the love and pleading of your daughter, old man."

"Don't make this any harder, baby girl. I'm trying to say that I'm sorry and I'm going to help."

A stuttering laugh erupted from my lips like a live volcano. "That's all I've been doing is making life easier for you and harder for me. Now, my life and the life of my kid were on the line and I don't have shit to show for it. Matter of fact, let me give you the same advice you gave me. Don't make my time with Gideon any harder or you wont have to worry about Keith or Farmer turning you in. I will. How do you like that allegiance?"

I hopped out of the ring and threw the gloves at Keith who was staring at us curiously. It was a small gym, but I knew in matters such as these it was better if everyone was deaf. People knew how to mind their business. Unless you made it their business like with my gym break up. I had no fears that my conversation with dad would travel beyond the red ropes.

"When did you stop believing that I'd protect you?" Pursing his lips, he leaned against the post of the ring breathing heavily. Looking a little worn out, like he could use a nap. Regarding me with sympathetic eyes.

I almost started to laugh again. The old man wasn't so spry after all. I remembered when I used to think that he would always be this inhuman robot, towering over me. Now I was the immature kid, wanting to kick the cane out of his grasp. But any sympathy built up in me was quickly stamped out. "When did you ever?"

"How about when the school wanted to press charges when you hit David and they didn't because I argued them down. In the end, we mutually settled on suspension. I've always had your back. I even knew that you had applied to some colleges at your counselor's encouragement. Which is why, when you didn't get accepted into any of the colleges of your choice I chucked the letters and forced you into boxing. I never wanted you to be disappointed. I'd rather you believe that I led you into something you weren't comfortable with than have you think that you weren't good enough at all."

I was speechless.

"I knew that without your mother I could never raise a girl. So if you had half a chance of turning out good and not a complete reckless slut. In my mind, I had to raise you as a boy. Some of my decisions passed inappropriately, but I'd do it all again. If it meant seeing you becoming this intelligent, fierce but beautiful young woman who loves her son and would do anything for her family."

"There's—" My words came to a halt as he talked over me.

"I'm not asking you to trust me. Just give me time to make this right. Not for Owen, but for my daughter. It's what she deserves."

"Oh, so the money and the fame ain't got the same pull it used to." Unable to pass up the opportunity to snap at him.

"I don't want to lose my family."

"Does that family include Auntie Shannon now? Because according to Gideon it didn't. And don't think I didn't tell her about that."

"My sister-in-law and I exchanged words. She reminded me that my wife would be disappointed in how I was treating everyone. Her heart was big enough to hold the world. It's about time that I start carrying her memory in a way that she might actually approve of. In a way that my daughter would actually be proud of. I haven't had a chance to be your daddy in a long time."

I inhaled loudly and slowly released a deep breath. A heaviness in my body that told me I needed a hug. At least before my headache set in. "Did you bring your car? Can you take me home?"

"Yeah," he nodded. Slowly climbing out of the ring and handing the pads to Keith. Who was looking between us as if he had just witnessed something momentous, but wasn't sure what it was?

We didn't say anything else as I gathered my things. I really didn't need him to. My heart was just stuck in the past. While my brain was telling me that I had a chance for a new present. It was hard to believe that any of this was happening. Everything in my life had taken this weird turn. Except for Owen, he was my one constant.

"Maybe we could all have dinner together sometime?" my dad asked me.

Pushing the strap of my gym bag higher on my shoulder, I shook my head vehemently. "No that's not a good idea. Neither is Grandparent's Day. Not until you can prove that your family matters more than boxing."

Only to look over into the eyes of Mark, who looked like he had been waiting for me. I put my head down and tried to go around him, but he wasn't going to give up that easily.

"Michelle, can we talk?"

"This guy bothering you," my dad spoke up. Like a Pitbull waiting for the word to bite his arm off.

I handed him my gym bag which was mostly just a backpack and said, "Can you pull the car around?"

"Let me try to explain what you heard? I don't want you to think any of what I said was true."

I held up the palm of my hand. "Save it. All the men in my life have proven to be liars at one time or another. Blood may lead me to forgive my father. But nothing is going to make me ignore what you said. It took me a lifetime to get rid of Darren. I don't want his little brother."

My father blared the horn for me to come out.

"Just listen—"

Despite my need to make a scene, I kept my voice perfectly under control. "You can forget the classes. The greatest thing you taught me is that I can give myself to someone and it still not be enough. And I am sorry that I was not enough."

Turning on a dime to leave him behind. Focused on stopping my father's incessant blaring. I guess one thing hadn't changed and it was his patience. Getting into the car, I slammed the door shut. Looking angrily ahead.

"Okay, well if you had answered the blare sooner. I would have told you that I forgot my cell phone. Now I've got to go back and get it. Just hold on."

He went back inside and I sighed heavily. Thinking how much cooler my walkout would have been if we had just pulled off. I pressed the radio on and it didn't immediately come off. Dad's car was old-school and responded to a little abuse. I hit the top of it and then hit the button again with the side of my fist. Not only was the music blaring, but the glove box flew open and dad's phone fell out. I looked back at the entrance peculiarly as he came out, took out the phone, and closed the box back.

"You getting forgetful, old man."

"Don't tell anyone," he grinned, pocketing the phone before pulling off.

Chapter 23

Throwing my bag on my bed, I quickly shower and change, and plop down on the couch. My auntie made herself scarce after she found out that dad drove me home. Her hands clenching and unclenching as if she just might rearrange his face just by breathing the same air as him. It wasn't as if I had invited him up. But I was looking forward to being alone. So I didn't contradict her anger.

Today had been taxing. I was forced to confront Mark about his hurtful lies. My dad wants to become an instant supportive family. He's decided that our mutual enemy should bring us together. In his head, he was already the hero and overdue for forgiveness. Thankfully, I could swat his vibrato down with a broomstick, now that I had found my voice. And I still had to speak to Owen about keeping secrets from me. Even if his outings with my dad had been innocent enough.

But I wasn't watching TV. The TV was watching me. It felt like I had to crack a safe and beyond the vault were all my feelings for Mark. But if I opened it then I would become shattered glass. A big girl crying on the floor of my bedroom. I had to make a better effort than that for Owen. So instead, the TV had been watching me for at least 2 hours now.

"Mom, it's your song."

"What?"

"It's your song," he said ecstatically as he came and grabbed my hand. Pulling me up from the couch by pure force of will. I laughed at his antics. Unable to imagine what could have him riled up like this.

It wasn't my favorite song, but it was the one that I had told him I played at my last fight. Apparently, in this game they let your character listen to the radio. He turned the TV up so that I could hear True by Amaranthe better. I smiled at him knowingly, realizing that this was his way of cheering me up. Sons can be very observant and tricky.

But before I could protest. He was jumping up and down in his bed in his socks. Bolting out the guy parts like he was in the band. That was all she wrote. I jumped in. After all, this was a duet. Pounding my feet on the bed with the enthusiasm of a 16-year-old girl. Holding my son's hand as we bounced around and fell down. Ending the song halfway out of breath and leaning against his twin-sized headboard.

"You know what would be cooler than this?"

Ice cream, I predicted. Allowing him time to get to the point. Resisting the urge to ask him how he knew that I needed the pick me up. Especially when that might lead to questions like, what upset me in the first place? And I wasn't comfortable with talking about any of this with my underage son. Who thought it was silly that I needed a nightlight, but still believed that his closet was haunted. Thanks to a poorly done joke by my father some odd years ago when we first moved in.

"Can Mark come to my next debate? The desert run after is optional," He grinned. "I could use the support."

His words threw me off guard, my smile faltering. The fact that he had taken so well to the man would be almost endearing if it wasn't so cruel. But the meaning of his last words struck me as odd. "You know that I support you in all you do right?"

"Yeah and so does grandpa. It's just nice having another guy around."

"Then he will be there," I replied with half a grin. Was it possible to still send messages by carrier pigeon? I guess email was the next best thing. Talking to that man would have me biting my tongue until it bled in order to not curse him out or cry.

I lost the latter battle later that night at bedtime. My only entertainment was the tile on my ceiling. There was nothing else to distract me. Only my thoughts were left. And I didn't want to be alone with them in the dark. I thought I had found my prince charming and he was only a toad. But for a minute I knew what it was like to be appreciated and loved. Why can't I hold on to that feeling permanently? What makes me so undeserving? Was Boxing killing my love life? Or was I the problem all along? I didn't have a fairy Godmother appearing in my room to deliver all the answers. I'd be lucky enough to find a therapist to unravel the mystery of my never-ending mistakes. Or a chemist to change my pheromones that seem to only attract shitty dudes.

Twenty minutes in and enough snot bubble sobs to disgust my auntie if she were here. My eyelids felt gummy from hot tears. I even became disgusted with myself. My favorite blanket doubling as a Kleenex. Sniveling like a child as I wiped my nose. But I never wanted to be this pitiful. Seeking out my only source of happiness. Which meant sneaking into Owen's room to snuggle next to him.

"Mom," he groaned, his voice thick with sleep.

"I'm scared of the dark," I hiccuped, wrapping my arms around him as he fell back to sleep. That wasn't exactly a lie either. My flat monotone voice was dead even to my ears.

Which was fine, because it would match my heart. It was starting to feel dead to love.

A week later was Owen's debate. And for once I didn't have a fight that day. So I was able to catch a ride with Auntie Shannon. Running back to her car to retrieve her sweater for her. Everyone was already inside. Even my dad and Darren showed up.

At least tonight, I was here on time and ready to play the perfect dutiful parent. What the PTA considers the perfect parent anyway. I only had one respectable dress and I wore that already. So this time, I threw a leather jacket on over it and some gym shoes. And my best don't fuck with me, smile. I should get through this all right.

At least that was the plan before I ran into Mark in the parking lot. My heart pounding in my chest as if my very soul recognized him.

"Hi."

"Hey."

We both walked in together. And for a second I wasn't sure if I was following him or if he was following me. It's not like we both haven't been here before, but it was clear that things were more than a little awkward. Throwing each other goofy smiles and giggles that filled the air like wind chimes. I felt like a girl with a crush. Instead of a woman whose heart was recovering from a Haymaker. There was clearly undeniable sexual tension between us, but now I knew better.

"Michelle, maybe we can talk after all this?"

"Talk about what, Mark? Your misunderstanding, because on top of not being a real woman I'm also deaf. I didn't really hear the things that I did. Stop it. You said what you said. It never should have come out of your mouth in the first place. But now that it has, how can I look at you the same? You are clearly the douchenozzle I always thought you were."

Ring the bell, that was a TKO. I hit him where it hurts with nothing, but the truth. Why would he think that explaining his words away as nothing more than a misunderstanding would ever make things right? The right thing would have not to have said them at all. I don't know how I could ever trust him with me, again. Apparently, I wasn't woman enough like Caliece to withstand the truth.

"Mark, you're here!" Owen exclaimed, running into the man's arms.

The frown that formed on Darren's lips took me by surprise. As does the indifference gracing my fathers. He'd never been formally introduced to Mark as a boyfriend or otherwise. And he seemed to be the least interested out of the whole group. Something was clearly up because he never took a hands-off approach to my relationship.

"You know my Auntie and this is my father and his friend Darren."

"Nice to meet you all," he answered, giving my aunt a quick hug. Before going up to the men to shake their hands. Of course, Darren refused to shake his hand and he merely smirked. Stepping back so as not to make a scene in front of Owen. My father looked on approvingly at the pissing match.

I scowl at him, not surprised that he's avoiding the heat from my gaze. Obviously, things between me and Mark were past done, but I don't need this right now. Dad had to get used to me dating other people. Or maybe not because I smell like loser juice and I'm only attracting dogs.

Nodding, I try to contain my disappointment at the whole thing. "Why don't we all take our seats."

"Owen, you're needed backstage."

I kissed the top of his head, good luck, and watched as he ran over to his teacher. Following her backstage. The house lights went off, and everyone's talking reduced to a low murmur.

I grabbed my aunt's hand and whispered, "sit next to me."

However, when we got to the aisle. My dad tugged on her hand viciously and practically pulled her out of the seat. Leaving me stuck between Mark and Darren. If we weren't at an elementary school right now. I'd be cussing him out. Although, I wasn't sure if Mark noticed that anything was off.

"Thank you all for coming," began Owen's debate teacher.

I exhaled loudly and rolled my shoulders back and forth. Settling in for the awkwardness. A tension in my lower back that was making it uncomfortable to sit in these chairs. I looked over when Mark cleared his throat. Our shoulders touched in a way that I could feel his strength and warmth. The same warmth that I found solace in only two weeks ago.

Leaning over, his melon-flavored breath brushed my cheek, "You're right, there is no good excuse. I never should have said what I did."

Nodding, to avoid the need to kiss him and taste the flavor.

"SSShh, the boys coming on. Rude much," Darren said, leaning over to look Mark directly in his eyes.

I almost elbowed him in the gut, when he put his hand on the back of my chair like we were together. This was the first time that he had ever been at one of Owen's events. And It hadn't escaped my notice that his first time is conveniently a week after he finds out about me dating Mark.

I pulled out my phone and tried to text my dad.

Michelle: If I had told you that Mark and I had broken up. Would you still have pulled a stunt like this?

His phone began to ring obnoxiously. Drawing the pissed-off gazes of a few parents from the rows in front of us. Turning around to shame him into cutting it off. I almost laughed, putting my cell on vibrate as etiquette dictates. Dad – 0, PTA - 1. Only for it to vibrate two minutes later.

Dad: You and Mark were dating? I didn't know that.

Now it was my turn to lean over and try to catch his gaze. His eyes were glued on the stage as if they were watching the fight of the century. I reluctantly sat back and threw a glance at Darren. This man couldn't wait to sing to my dad. His smile was loving. It threw me for such a loop, I almost gave the man my bag. Clearly this stranger actually capable of smiling and meaning it was here to rob me. Turning my body away from him, I put one leg over the other and angled towards Mark. His spicy scent doing things to my nether regions that I didn't need reminding of. I pursed my lips and moved to the edge of my seat. The things you do for your kid.

As soon as Owen gets to the podium, I stood up obnoxiously and clapped my hands. So loudly they even started to burn. Hooping and hollering like I was at a concert before my auntie reached over to pull me down. I really needed the temporary reprieve from all that testosterone.

"What are you doing?" Darren's hostile voice was almost inviting. At least that was what I was used to. Not the niceties he was throwing at me in order to impress Mark.

"Supporting my son, what are you doing?"

Frowning, he placed his hands on top of mine. "Supporting you."

"I've entered the Twilight Zone, haven't I."

My auntie snickered behind her hand. Only to draw the weary gaze of my father who was conveniently out of the loop.

Sliding Darren's hand gently off of mine. I tried once again to focus on Owen's debate.

"Well said Owen, and the winner of this round of debates goes to Owen Nunn for presenting the argument against the use of coal.

"It's over. Woah, God, that was beautiful," I declared, standing up once more to applaud. Scattered applause from tired parents was sprinkled throughout the crowd. As the lights are turned up and parents head to the door to leave. It wasn't hard to spot the helicopter parents who were making an instant beeline for their student's teachers. At least the ones who were obligated to attend.

I maneuvered my way around Darren and laced my arms with my aunt. Using her as a human shield. "Wasn't Owen positively great?"

"I wouldn't expect nothing less from a kid from my bloodline," my father replied beautifully.

Auntie Shannon patted the top of my hand and I almost wanted to collapse against her. Like you don't know how hard this is. Instead, we both turned as Owen came running toward us. But Darren stepped in like an oncoming freight train. To lift the boy off his feet and even I had to laugh.

"You did awesome little buddy."

He laughed, but at some point, he must have had enough because he made a swipe at the man's face. Forcing Darren to end his faux stepdaddy moment. I was almost proud of my little bugger. This certainly called for a double scoop of ice cream. I looked around for Mark to see if he saw the same thing I did and he was already gone. I sighed and relinquished the grip on my aunt's arm.

I wish I knew what a real apology sounded like.

Chapter 24

Half listening to Owen's recount of his speech that he likens to playing Call Of Duty. I know I need to talk to my father. These kinds of backhanded dealings can't go unchecked. I'm sick of the men in my life going back on their promises to me. When did people become so untrustworthy?

"I'm going to say goodbye to dad before we leave," I tell Auntie Shannon, who was just buckling up her seatbelt.

"Will wait for you."

I laugh when without missing a beat Owen compares a crash he had on the game to walking on stage. Clutching his small trophy as if it might never leave his hand.

"Hurry back mom."

"Of course." Closing the door softly, I headed across the small parking lot toward my dad. He was standing outside of Darren's car taking a smoke break. The parking lot was dark except for the light drifting in from people's headlights. Darren, no doubt, was still inside trying to get some poor unsuspecting teacher's phone number. I can't believe my dad chose him over me, again. I'm starting to get that pain never goes away even if you know it's coming.

"Don't start little girl," he said, putting out his half-smoked cigarette on the side mirror. The ashes fall to the ground. "Darren will be out any minute. These pretentious assholes would love to witness a scene to put on book face."

"Good, I don't want to speak to Darren. I just want to hear from you. What was the plan? Outside of embarrassing me in front of my son. Have you conveniently forgotten that little speech you gave me two weeks ago in the ring?"

He shook his head and pulled out his cigarette pack, placing the shrunken bud in the pack. The smell of cigarettes already starting to tickle the back of my throat.

"Then you go and pull this bullshit. Not only do you not tell me that Darren is coming, but I didn't even know you would be here. And you make it so that Darren is sitting next to me and not Auntie Shannon. Still under the impression that you can make decisions for me. When I made it extremely clear that you can't. I'm not getting back with Darren and fuck you for trying to make me."

His silence is so maddening that it only adds lighter fluid to the fire. Glancing towards the front door of the school, ready to scatter back to Auntie Shannon's car like a wild raccoon at the mere sight of Darren. Shooting him a glare that could slice through him. But he simply stared. He doesn't yell, coerce or try to grab me. It was like I was ready for a fight that would never come. Stuck in the changing room ready for someone to knock on my door.

"I'm not with Mark...anymore. He came to support Owen because my little boy wanted him there. That's the only man in my life who matters. And you ruining his moment with your juvenile shit is uncool. Darren's the fakest, guy, I've ever met. Tonight just confirmed that."

"Agreed." My dad's voice is low and somber and I'm almost taken aback. His scratchy cigar voice soothed my nerves.

"We're actually in agreement."

"I'm new at this change thing. And I know that's no excuse either. It's just fact." He pocketed the cigarettes and leaned back against the car. "I mean right now I'm sure he's in there slobbering on some teacher."

I laughed. "Right?"

"He managed to convince me that he had changed his ways like me and that he wanted to make it work with you for real. I didn't know much about this Mark guy. So I figured what the hell. I'll invite him to Owen's event. And in the future, you will see me at this boring stuff more. But tonight I realized that you'll never find the right guy with me pulling the puppet strings. You do deserve better than Gideon and Darren and that baby daddy of yours. I had green-colored glasses on. Now they're off. That cool little boy of yours helped me kick it. The boxing world just ain't good enough for us anymore."

Raising an eyebrow at him, I said, "It's a shit ton of money thanks to pay-per-view."

"That's why you're not losing this fight."

Oh, I mouthed with my lips. No sound coming out.

"It's one of the reasons. Come on, you'd certainly make more if you lost. Don't twist my words."

I guess that was a start for him.

Suddenly, the car chirped indicating that Darren was making his way over. "Get out of here before he sees you. I'll let the jerk down easy. Family matters."

I kissed him quickly on the side of his cheek. The scruff of his beard scratched my top lip. Before I rushed back to Auntie Shannon's car.

Who teasingly reminded me of the traffic lining up to flee this place. But even she couldn't stop smiling at our father/daughter moment. We don't get many. But when they were great. They were awesome. I couldn't wait to see what the future held.

Without dance, my future was getting pretty dim. Farmer was still out of the loop on the real plan for fight seven. For him, this fight was the culmination of all our hard work. So he was taking my training seriously. I still hadn't made up my mind whether to believe dad or not. But I had 12 rounds to figure it out. So I was buckling down on my training as well.

But I missed smiling with Mark. I missed our laughter. Everything in my life these days was so grueling. I was even taking to running up and down the stairs of my apartment 5 times to build up my endurance. Now, Farmer, had me sparring with him around the building. Walking backward as I tried to stay on point and hit my marks. It was like I traded in my heels for some purple Carrera Runners.

My body badly craved some downtime sitting on the couch with Mark and Owen just watching a bad movie. Instead, I got, Gideon, coming in to watch me train. His presence filled the gym like a storm cloud. Only to remind me that I'm supposed to lose this fight. Signing my life away on a suspicious-looking document. My dad just shook his head and reminded me to go along to get along. Afterward, I took a Peach Cinnamon Protein break just to calm down and shake the madness from my day.

For everything to be so right. It still all felt wrong.

And it had been at least 4 weeks now since I'd broken up with Mark. When were things going to feel normal again?

"I'm just worn out, blank," I said heading into the changing room with her. Dropping my bag on the shaggy carpeting.

"Are you stressin' over the fight? Or are you stressin' because you miss your guy?" she asked leaning over the sink and removing her makeup from this morning.

I sat on the chair, unable to even change into my workout gear. My muscles literally too exhausted to move. "Both."

She nodded as if she understood. "Being heartsick can sometimes make you physically sick. Wow, you must really love this guy?"

I shook my head. "Nah, I got too much to do."

She came to stand in front of my changing room and I was almost tempted to slide my curtain closed.

"Your body is saying you do." She looked me over with concern. "I've been watching you train for this fight. Dare I say it's starting to look a little excessive."

I gave her a half-smile. "You better not let Gideon hear you say that. Or maybe he'd like it. He's sending mixed signals these days."

"I'm surprised, I'm saying that. So it will probably never happen again," she said wide-eyed. Going back to the mirror to take her makeup off. "But the easiest solution to one of those problems is to just talk to him."

"I can't. It wasn't my mistake. He doesn't even think I'm a real woman. Just an imposter until the real women like Caliece shows up."

"Admittedly, I didn't think this dance thing was a good idea. But even I can't understand why he would say that. It's such a stereotype that somehow we're harsher or more demanding. Some men are just idiots. You want me to talk to him?"

At that, I closed the curtain's in a huff, "No. I don't need my bestie solving my problems."

"If you say so."

I can hear her moving into the changing room. The sound of her curtain closing beside me. I bit my lip and lowered my voice. "Of course, if you could tell Farmer you're sparring with me today instead of him. It might give me a little break."

She laughed. "What are friends for?"

I smiled, at least I had a better track record making friends than I did dating.

She finished changing before me. "I'll meet you downstairs okay."

"All right."

An hour of procrastination later, I exited the changing room as a group of students was going in. With way more energy than I could muster just being in the same room with them. Only to stop in my tracks at the sight of Mark talking to Madam Bellamy, the owner of the dance studio. I only recognized her because of her picture hanging in the hall. But whatever news she was delivering must've been upsetting.

She looked positively regal doing it. Her silver-grey hair with hints of the blond it used to be was stunning. Pulled up out of her face with a butterfly clip. She looked like the type of woman to drop a hanky and expect you to pick it up. Like yes, she still carries hankies and everyone in the world is her servant.

"I'm sorry, Mark, but it looks like you will have to find a new partner for the competition."

He saw me out of the corner of his eye but didn't say anything. Instead, he just stormed out. A part of me wanted to chase after him, but it wasn't my place.

I could see the contention she might cause in Farmer's former marriage. Considering everyone in the boxing world as low-bred when clearly she was a queen. Her daughter was automatically born with a silver spoon in her mouth. If expensive wine was a real person then it would probably look like her. Yet, I approached her as a woman who didn't care.

"I'm sorry ma'am for eavesdropping," I said tapping her on the shoulder and shaking her hand a little more roughly than I intended. "I'm Michelle Nunn, I box downstairs, but I also took one of Mark's classes."

"I know who you are."

Well, that was a little off-putting. It offered up some questions that I knew I wouldn't get the answers to. Did my reputation proceed me? Or were Mark and Farmer more talkative than I give them credit for? "Mark spoke about the competition often. Did I hear you correctly? Caliece dropped out?"

The woman rubbed her hands together as if she were devastated at the news. "No, darling, she didn't drop out. She made Edguardo her partner."

The woman looked pleasantly over her shoulder. "With the competition in two days, he could use a friend right now."

I immediately shook my head. "Oh, I don't think——-"

"Don't think child. I know more about what goes on here than you." She tapped my shoulder before heading into Studio 3.

I looked back to the double doors where I could see Mark taking a break through the glass window. He could use a friend, but I could've used an understanding boyfriend. I bit my lower lip and turned and walked away. There was grueling work to be had. I had a fight in two days.

Heading downstairs, I smirk at the sight of Brooke sneaking a small paper into the suggestion box on top of the receptionist's desk. Who even reads that thing? It can't be Farmer and Gideon. I once suggested that they put in a water fountain at our old place and got the stare down of my life. Hmmm, maybe it was the owner of the dance studio. We clearly, had new lockers downstairs because of her. What else did she know?

"Yo, where did you go?"

"What?" I asked, putting my bag away and looking into the face of my bestie.

"I said, Farmer agreed to let me spar with you. I think he was a little preoccupied anyway. But so were you just now. Where did you go?"

"Brooke, Mark just got some bad news. And I kinda want to be there for him. But the reason I'm not is not my choice. I just feel silly ignoring the owner's advice."

She scrunched up her nose. "Gideon's giving out relationship advice now."

"No," I laughed. "The owner of the dance studio."

"The painting on the wall that looks like it belongs in a museum in the Victorian section." She shook her head. "You can ignore that."

"Be serious."

"If he can't accept you for who you are. Then how are you supposed to be there for him at his worse? Let that man cry you a river."

She helps me into my gloves and I look back over my shoulder to see Mark venturing into my world. "Why is he down here?" I whispered to Brooke.

"Oh yeah, it seems as if they will now be offering half-off memberships to the dance teachers if they want to work out. Seems like this temporary move just became permanent."

I looked back at him as he moved about the gym. Looking like he fits right in. My heart beat to the music of his every step. Imagining myself running my tongue over his abs before he snapped me into his arms where he knew I belonged.

"I'm not going to survive this new arrangement."

"Don't worry fight seven is right around the corner and after that, you get a vacay and who doesn't need that."

Me. I just want Mark.

Chapter 25

"This is your shot. You don't have time to squander it. She wants your belt. She wants your crown. But she ain't you. She ain't trained like you. She ain't been through what you been through. So how can she stand in that ring and say she is the next one to wear that belt?" Farmer belted, just before he gave me my headphones.

"It's a lot of money, love. But you got to love yourself after it's all said and done. So don't hang your hat on some belt or any money. Just fight your fight." My aunt told me before she left with Owen to take their seats.

"I've got this under control. Just fight the match you want," My dad whispered into my ear every five minutes.

"Your family is on the line. Lose this fight," Gideon reminded me as soon as I set my foot on the pavement.

"The love of your life is fighting his own battle across town. This one is about yours. I already know you got this. Go and make history," Brooke touted as she helped me get ready.

"Can everyone just get out of here? I need time to think. Alone." I cleared the packed room in twenty minutes. It was like everyone and their mama wanted to be a witness to the moment. But there was no moment. It was just me trying to get my heart under control. Long enough for my brain to tell me what to do when I step into the ring. I finally got to rest for two days. Much of which I spent dragging Owen out of school because I was so worried about what would happen to him the closer we got to Bout day. The media outside the room was so thick that it would choke a Giraffe.

I flipped frantically through my phone trying to find that song True, that had gotten lost in the shuffle. Instead, I was stuck on Lose to Win by Fantasia.

However, instead of calming me down, I was going into a panic. Gideon's words played in my head to lose. My father reminded me that I didn't have to. Even my aunt gave me permission to lose as if that's ever an option. Compounded by the fact that I wasn't the only one losing today. So was Mark. It was just too much on my mind that I ended up screaming.

A quick rapt came at the door seconds later.

I exhaled, just knowing that I brought the Calvary back to my door. "Who is it?"

Brooke came with a huge grin on her face. "You got to see this."

I looked at the huge crowd of media behind her. Remembering the times when it was just a handful. Now I had to weigh the importance of whether the push through the cameras was worthy of this news.

Sensing that she groaned, "Come on this might even make the news."

I frowned. "That's not enticing at all."

Still, I followed her outside. My headphones were still on my ear as it played the song on repeat. Hoping to drown them out, but really I was just drowning. Painfully aware of the screaming cameras like background music to my anxiety. Allowing us just enough room to pass and not much more. It felt like I was a sardine in one of those cans that peel back. I was beginning to curse Brooke and hoped that this was worth it.

A few screaming fans interrupted the throng to tell me how much they loved me and my relationship with Owen. That gave me a temporary boost. Almost ruined by the flash of camera bulbs that were making it hard for me to see my feet. Brooke grabbed my hand and pushed through a little more forcefully.

Only to stop in front of a construction site going on next door. Except at 7 pm at night, it was closed down. Leaving me to wonder just what Brooke was so frantic about. Meeting a homeless fan would make the news, but I didn't need that kind of publicity. Losing this fight was going to be enough. But what I saw was Brooke's headlights shining across a green tarp snapped to the poorly erected gate. Intended to keep rift raft out when really it was just a deterrent to people who already knew better. But there was something spray-painted in white across it.

I stepped in front of her car to read the whole thing and almost cried. Brooke served as an impromptu bodyguard in order to keep everyone back long enough for me to read it. "How did you know this was here?"

"I got a friendly tip."

Mark spray painted, 'Holy shit, I love you' across the front of the tarp in white. Outside, of him being the only man in my life who would ever write something like that. He also signed his first name underneath it in cursive. That man certainly lived dangerously.

Brooke came up to me. "You know what you want to do?"

My dad came through the thicket, very much annoyed. "What the hell is going on here? The fight is inside. Michelle Nunn versus Amber Spence."

"Dad," I called to him, stepping out of Brooke's supportive grasp.

He frowned as he read the tarp.

"Please dad, take me to him."

"You're going to lose this fight," he replied quietly.

"Doesn't matter."

"It's a lot of money."

I looked at Brooke, knowing she would be my backup if needed, but I really wanted to take this ride with my dad.

"$90,000 isn't a bad start in life. So what do you say?"

He grimaced. "So was $450,00, but I'll bring the car around."

Brooke hopped up and down. "Since this fight is clearly over. I'm coming too."

I grabbed her hand. My thoughts raced as the words of that song finally registered. Sometimes you do have to lose to win again. "Tell my Auntie and Owen what's happening. I don't want them to worry, but I still have to go get my things."

"Michelle, are you going to finish this fight? Who is Mark? Was that message meant for you? Is there a story behind that?" I threw the headphones off and hung them around my neck. In the midst of deciding that I didn't mind losing this fight if it meant winning Mark.

Getting back to my room, I quickly packed my things. Not at all confident enough to run into Farmer or Keith right now. But I wasn't fast enough because Gideon burst into the room. Did my room suddenly have the words, open season on the front? Sure, that he had heard what was happening from the throng outside.

"Don't be upset. I'm still losing the fight right?"

He pushed me up against the wall. My head banging against the plaster. "You expect me to believe that small fire in my office wasn't you. Which conveniently sent your contract up in flames before the sprinklers came on."

I hit him in his jaw. It felt like stone and I knew I'd be bruising tonight, but it was enough to send him stumbling back. Before I kicked him between the balls. Sending him crouching towards the ground. "I expect you to believe that I don't know what the fuck you talking about."

"I'm going to fucking waist you for this."

Before I could even think about what else to do. My dad came bursting. Kicking the door closed with his shoe as he pulled out a gun. "What's going on?"

"I figured he'd come in here after finding my little gift."

"Okay, but I took care of him," I said pointing at Gideon who had yet to get up from the floor. Shooting us both evil glares. As if he were already picturing our burials. I bet he even had his own plot of land. Some no-name place out in the suburbs, where all the bodies go. Where ours would end up. "Put the gun down, dad. It's over."

"With men like this, there is no such thing as over. He's not going to end at some charred contract."

I bit my bottom lip, unable to combat the truth.

"So you just get out of here. There's a boy waiting on you."

My heart weighed heavy with everything he was asking me. A fear in the pit of my stomach that I had only felt once before when I was being robbed. Except, I wasn't worried about my life. I was worried about my father. No one can walk away from a decision like this. And I couldn't walk away from the man who was about to make it. "We can figure this out, dad."

"I already have. And you promised me that you would let me fix it. So go now. That boy wont wait forever."

I wanted to chide him on calling Mark a boy. But I realized that he wasn't talking to me per se. He was talking to little girl, me. In his mind, he was a father protecting his little girl. This wasn't my decision to make for him. It was the one decision that he had to make for me.

"I'm going to draw the cameras away. I never saw you come in with the gun," I said, throwing my bag over my shoulder.

"Fucking, bitch," Gideon barked, spitting on my shoe.

I didn't even look down at him. How could I still be able to walk away? I just stared at my father's unwavering hand as the gun was aimed at the man's head. Pursing my lips, I bridged the gap between us. Stopping beside him, I leaned over to kiss him on the cheek.

"I made you. Who is Michelle Nunn without Gideon behind her?"

"Whatever I want," I sighed, and grabbed my father's free hand. It was curled so tightly into a fist, you couldn't squeeze a penny between his thumb and forefinger.

I exited without showing too much of what was going on inside. "I'm not fighting tonight. There is a guy who needs me more."

A few minutes ago that might have even been true. But I still had to walk away with plausible deniability. The reporters asked tons of questions, as they followed me like little ducklings being led away by their mother. Waddling with heavy cameras in their hand.

"Why are you quitting? Are you afraid you're going to lose to Amber 'Shatterproof' Spence? Does this change of heart have to do with the sign outside? Everyone's depending on you, why leave?"

I turn once I'm safely outside to address them. Marveling at my own coning. "Everyone that matters, wants me to do this. To my fans, I'm sorry. Amber will be a great champion."

Brooke ran up to me. "Hey, I saw your dad go back inside. Looks like he might have had a change of heart. Do you need a ride?"

"Yeah, I don't know what he's thinking." I got into the car to see my Auntie and son already in the back. Their enthusiasm at this impromptu getaway filled the car and threatened to chase away my blues. Their comforting hands on my shoulder gave me strength. Fighting the urge to turn back and fight my dad's stupid plan. I swallowed the lump in my throat and looked back at the place. Dad.

Chapter 26

Thirty minutes later, we were pulling up in front of the Grand Ballroom Chicago. The place looked paltry on the outside. Huge beautiful windows were reminiscent of days long past. When men wouldn't be caught dead outside without a suit and the women always wore dresses. The building was large and unassuming. The smell of gyros drifting over to us from a small restaurant on the corner. If it wasn't for the small red carpet lining the entrance. A huge guard out in front who looked like he could sub for one of the doormen of the Emerald City in The WIZ. Wearing a green suit jacket with black pants. He didn't actually look bad either.

Neither did he stop and ask questions. He opened the door as soon as we approached as if he were my fairy Godfather and he just knew I belong inside. Not bothering with my attire. Even though I was still in a plain white top and black shorts for the fight. A black sports bra underneath. But if the guard's attire didn't make me question my appearance. Everyone else did.

The place was packed with people. Dancers, judges, spectators. Most of the dancers had numbers attached to their backs and teams on their heels. Makeup artists and seamstresses were being shouted instruction. Finding Mark in this would be all, but impossible. And

I was already starting to draw the disdainful looks of some of the spectators. Whispering at the sight of a degenerate among so much class. I turned to face Brooke and Auntie Shannon who stood behind me. "This—"

"—is not your chance to back down," Brooke finished for me.

"Yeah, mom you're going to look so cool dancing with Mark. I'm not sure about Mark though," Owen chimed in earnestly.

My auntie popped him lightly on the arm. And I almost started to laugh.

"I was wondering when you would show up?" Madam Bellamy's thin dainty voice came up behind me.

I turned around in shock.

"I've heard a great deal about you from Farmer and Mark and you come highly esteemed. I assumed most of it was greatly exaggerated. But your appearance here tonight says something else. Mark is my best boy."

I folded my hands in front of me, politely. Feeling like I was in the presence of a queen somehow. The fact that I had made it onto her radar and it wasn't for hitting Mark was a positive in my opinion. Especially a woman as regal as she looked in a grey satin gown that twirled loosely at her feet. The sleeves were translucent. She snapped her fingers, and a whole team appeared from the crowd of passerby's.

"You can't very well meet him looking like that."

My stomach dropped and it felt like my insides were quaking in their juices. A small hand, I assumed to be Owen's pushed me forward.

"She's ready," Auntie Shannon said behind my back.

"A true owner is prepared for any eventuality. Even an impromptu dress change. As Caliece appears to be fine. You can wear her backup dress."

I looked up at the blue garment bag that one of her helpers held up. Its contents were shrouded in mystery. "I don't think Caliece and I are the same size."

"Are you doubting what I do?"

Brooke leaned over and whispered, "I wouldn't doubt this one."

Madam Bellamy held out her hand and I placed mine on top of hers tentatively. Not sure how to behave. She led me back to some changing rooms. The floors were covered in glitter and it smelled like a mixture of too many performances. But it was a different kind of excitement than I had felt before my matches. The tone of which aired on the side of somberness. These women were excited and craved the thrill of the competition. It was like the moment just before a lion grabs its prey. Glorious. And I was a part of it.

Not one for wearing makeup. The eye shadow and mascara made my lids feel heavier and I found myself blinking rapidly. As Madam Bellamy stood by and dished out instructions. Pulling my hair out of its cornrows as it fell to my shoulders in a wispy wave. But I wasn't used to this much goodwill. "What's in this for you?"

"It's more about what I'm not losing," she answered honestly. "Caliece and Edguardo are in the final round, as are Mark and his stand-in. And they both represent Center Stage Dance Studio. So if you completely botch this. We still have a chance at the championship."

"But why miss the opportunity to be one couple down. After all, you haven't seen me dance," I griped.

"I trust Mark as a teacher," she said, coming up behind me after the makeup artist was finished. I lifted my chin and checked my face in the mirror. "But you are right, I have not seen you dance. So I consider this a gift to him. That way not everyone can say that I do not have a heart." She turned my face to her and I stared into her eyes clearly being measured. "You look beautiful."

I let out a breath, that I didn't know I was holding. "Thank you."

She clapped her hands together. "Let's get her into this dress people."

After some tugging and lots of tape. It was done, it fit, and I felt naked.

"It would be longer on her, but for you, it hits mid-calf. It is perfect."

They turned me around like a doll they were dressing and posing. Shoving me in front of the first available full-length mirror. My hands instinctively went over my ass which was covered in a navy blue silk. A split up the right side would give me more than enough leg to flaunt. The bodice was made of an intricate gold lace trim. It kind of reminded me of a dress that you might find on the Goddess of Love, Aphrodite. A bare midriff that showed off my 4 pack. The spaghetti straps were thin and delicate. Until it looked like willpower alone was keeping the garment attached to my body. I turned and the team bowed.

"We are not worthy," the makeup artist replied, her eyes to the ground.

"No, we are magicians," the seamstress replied, as he bowed. But I frowned, not sure if I should take the man's statement as a compliment or not. His eyes also turned to the grown. As if someone knighted me, princess when I was not looking.

"Final dance," Another contestant yelled, sending some of the girls into a frenzy to finish freshening up. Fanning their armpits and sticking pins into wayward strands of their hair.

Madam Bellamy clapped her hands. "You are wanted on the dance floor."

I swallowed the lump in my throat and merely followed some of the other dancers out. Coming to the edge of the dance floor that met with the spectator seating area. The hardwood floors shone like new pennies. Old chandeliers were a reminder of the history of the place. As they looked like they were put in during the 1920s. Giving off mobster royalty.

Somewhere behind me, I heard someone whistling. I turned to see Brooke sitting at a round table with my family. She stood up and waved. I blew them all kisses. Surprised when I saw my dad sitting next to Auntie Shannon. He made it. Maybe he didn't pull the trigger after all. This moment, really was perfect now.

But as the house lights went down and the music began to play I was painfully aware of the fact that I still hadn't located Mark. There were seven couples in this final round and I was feeling like a fish out of water. I had to get in the game and show how. So I began to stalk the floor, looking for my prey. For my mate.

And I spotted him doing a simple two-step. His movements stopped as soon as our eyes connected across the room. The breathy exhale of the singer reminded me that they were dancing to the song he had chosen for us. Tina Turner's Private Dancer, that sly fox. The stand-by turned and revealed herself to be the secretary of the dance studio. She grunted just as the saxophone hailed her exit. Slipping off as only a dancer would like we had planned this exchange the whole time.

I went around to the back of him and untied his tie.

"What are you doing?"

I tied it tight. So that he would be dancing blind. "I'm asking you to prove you trust me?"

I twirl around him. Lovingly touching his arm ever so slightly, like a wood nymph playing a game of hide and seek. Until he grasped onto me.

"Found you."

We launched into a closed dance hold. As if our separation might mean death for both of us. Dancing under the midnight stars in our minds. Glad that he still remembered our dance as he twirled me out and into a forward open promenade. I was following his lead as much as he was following mine and it was effortless.

He did a twirl of his own and I followed behind him. Our timing was on the nose as we went back into hold. Just two lovers by the river. Utilizing the dance floor as we twirled as one this time. A controlled Hurricane, that turned into a beautiful ballerina.

But he wasn't the only one who had to give a little trust. Clinging onto him as the song belted the words, Private Dancer. My feet around his waist and my hands around his shoulders. He twirled in a circle without touching me; setting me back on my feet as if I weighed nothing more than a petal. The crowd erupting into applause.

But this was my story. I was his private dancer. So as rehearsed, I twirled away from him looking devastated at all the dreams I had, but wouldn't achieve. But this was one emotion that I didn't have to fake. Recalling all the feelings that sent me into turmoil before the fight. Mark's supportive words in my head. Half of the dance was portraying the emotion necessary to make the viewer believe in the magic.

I fell back into his waiting arms as he led me away from that tur-moil, but always resistant to change. I flip over his back as he tried to hoist me up. Nothing more than a pretty pile on the floor as I buried my head in my arm. He twirled around me as I did him in the beginning. Reaching out for me, only to have me shrug his embrace. Until finally, he knelt in front of me. Picking me up as we rocked together. Standing to our feet together. I unraveled the tie around his eyes and let it fall to the ground. As we swept the room together as one being. Our arms were an extension of each other.

Lifting me up during the instrumental onto his shoulder. More accepting of the change as I sit happily and shoot both my legs up in the air. He even removed one hand and I didn't move an inch. Sliding down his back. I turned and embraced him from behind, and that's how we danced until the song ended. And when I looked up, we were the last couple standing.

"From Center Stage Dance Studio, Mark Wade, and Partner are the winner of the 2019 Discover Dance Championships."

We bowed. Together and apart. Something inside us drew us close until we end up collapsing in each other's arms again. The announc-er came over to place a large ribbon, homecoming style across our chests. The words in white glitter on the blue sashes read, first place.

He ran his hands along my cheek. Drawing my attention away from the photographer. "I never meant to say the things I said to Caliece."

I shook my head. "It doesn't matter now."

"No, you need to let me explain. Darren told me that you two were together. And I didn't believe him. But then you're father came and told me that you guys were working things out and not to interfere. I wanted to fight for you. That is why I went to Owen's event, but when

I saw you with him. That picture-perfect family, I didn't know how I could compete with that."

I sighed, as the announcer came over with a trophy as big as me. We held it up together as we took more photos.

"Just what does that have to do with what you said to Caliece?" I asked through clenched teeth.

Happy when the photographer gave us the thumbs up that he was finished. I placed the trophy down with a clunk. Sure that it was heavy enough to put a dent in the floor. I faced him with questions in my eyes that I was almost scared to hear the answers to.

"Nothing, I was just being selfish. Caliece told me she was leaving to work with Edguardo and I was trying to appease her. In the hopes, she would stay and she didn't. And I only made myself miserable. I've got two gym memberships now because of you. I missed you. Please, don't be mad."

I grabbed his hands. "How can I be mad at you when that was all I was doing? Half of our relationship was hidden from the world until fairly recently. If anyone would have asked me about you. I don't know what I would have said."

He shook his head. "You wouldn't have said the things I did. Perfect people don't do things like that."

I laughed.

"Now we invite all of our guests to come join us on the floor," The announcer declared.

I looked over as people slowly got up from their tables. Our song replayed as we swayed back and forth. Completely ignoring the trophy that was picked up by one of Madam Bellamy's minions. I looked back into Mark's gaze and kissed his laughing lips. Pretty sure that this was one moment in time that I would never forget.

Suddenly, sirens interrupt the friendly tranquil gathering. I look towards my dad as he approached with the rest of my family. "What have you done?"

Trying to avoid a scene as cops looked around the place. He kissed me on the cheek and whispered, "I'm gonna go, but you made me so proud tonight. That trophy was the only one you were meant to get tonight. Don't let anyone tell you any different."

Afterword

Thank you for reading, *The Bolo Dance*. I have a soft spot for women fighters. Some might consider her softer than most. Maybe, but that was intentional. Just because someone is physically strong doesn't mean they can't be mentally weak. Especially when forced into a situation beyond their control like boxing. She hated it, but she was good at it. That doesn't mean that it was...her. Hopefully, that makes sense.

If you enjoyed it, read the next in the novel, *The Parry Garden*, available wherever books are sold. Just search TRS BOOKS website or the search bar of your reading app for 'The Parry Garden'.

Want to know when I release new books? Here are some other ways to stay updated:

Sign up for my new releases e-mail, so you can find out about the next book as soon as it's available:

www.trsbooks.com/newsletter/

Keep reading for a preview of The Parry Garden, Amber and Andrew's love story, available now!

Book Playlist

The Bolo Dance

You can listen here on Spotify or search for trsbooks

Wanted Dead Or Alive by Bon Jovi

Let The Music Play by Shannon

Run To You by Bryan Adams

Shoulder Of Orion by Lazerhawk

Television Romance by Pale Waves

In The Heat Of The Night by Sandra

Head Over Heels by Tears For Fears

Heart Out by The 1975

True by Amaranthe

The Best by Tina Turner

Lose To Win by Fantasia

Private Dancer by Tina Turner

Discussion Questions

1. What is the meaning of the title, The Bolo Dance?

2. Do you think Mark would have still loved Michelle if she chose boxing?

3. Classify Darren's relationship with Michelle's father?

4. What are Mark's true feelings on female boxers?

5. Will Darren's career survive without Michelle's fame?

6. Do you think Michelle's father truly had a change of heart at the end of the story?

7. Will Michelle eventually go back to boxing after the book closes?

Excerpt: The Parry Garden

PROLOGUE

I broke up with my boyfriend, Manny, upside down in a Camaro. It was a brief moment of calm before the shit storm hit. But who can really pick a perfect moment to do these things? I unbuckled myself from the passenger side seat and fell to the floor. That was formerly the roof.

"Good, now you can unbuckle me. I can't get it. The steering wheel is pressing into my stomach."

I do as I was told trying to thank my lucky stars that we had gone unharmed. But at that moment, I just loathed Manny. "We are so over. If I so much as see your caller ID after this. I'm getting a restraining order."

"You can't be serious," he said, dropping like a log. His weight was so heavy that it seemed to rock the car back and forth. I didn't find his surprise at my statement amusing. His bad-boy ways were good enough to be its own Hans Memling painting and I was over it today. This was the last night that I would go home with bumps and bruises that I didn't get from a fight. A person who wasn't two sheets to the wind was not supposed to be having these types of misadventures.

"Over, the end, complete, never to begin again."

Manny met my gaze, this time with a glare that would make me laugh under different circumstances. His side of the window was completely crushed. There was no way to get out on that side. My window was busted out and I most definitely smelled oil. With some degree of nausea, I made the painstaking climb through the window. Smelling like alcohol from the bottle that had burst on impact. Helping Manny secure his release after a jagged edge from the split cup holder snagged at his jacket. Scratching his hands on the glass to the point where he was drawing blood.

"Are you okay?" I asked once he was completely free.

"Never better."

It wasn't lost on me that this accident had immediately sobered him up. His red eyes were the only evidence that he had been drinking enough alcohol to induce a coma. Or that he had left the party with his keys leaving behind a four-body pile-up after he started a fight. Forcing me into the car because if we walked then he was pretty sure I'd end up going home with someone else. For all the sense that makes. The sirens got louder.

"I'm testifying against you," I admitted. "You put my life in danger. I'm your hostage."

He smacked his lips, running his hands over his five. "You had two drinks and you smell like how I feel. No one's going to believe that Shatterproof coming off her epic win is innocent."

His words took all the wind out of my sails. Marveling that he could actually summon tears for my brand new car. Running his hands through his blond highlighted hair so much that it was positively sticking up. I wanted to yell that it wasn't his car to cry over, but mine. Right, it was mine. Would they even believe that I wasn't the one driving? Thanks to Manny's antics, I had developed a reputation that wasn't wholly true.

A wild child with the need for speed and adventure.

Maybe when I first got with him that was what I wanted. Squinting my eyes at him as he kicked the tires with his low-top Christian Louboutin's as if that were enough to right my car. How drunk was he still? A car that we went together to get, but it became clear that it wasn't my dream purchase. It was his. Taking over the conversation with the salesman. But that truth wasn't going to get me out of this either. I had nothing to do with knocking over that stop sign. Narrowly missing a woman in the crosswalk and skipping like five red lights. But I smelled like the brewery at Bud Light and I had two heavy drinks that were still sitting on my stomach even now. And my reputation was going to kill me.

Red and blue lights finally made it to our block. A small quiet neighborhood that we were uprooting at three a.m. in the morning. Heads peeked out of closed curtains. Where even were we? How much was this lawyer going to cost me?

"Run," Manny suddenly blurted. The lights and sounds brought him out of his daze.

"What?"

"Fucking, run?" He repeated heading towards a house and the backyard. A gate was left open.

I looked around, clearly not ready for the criminal life. Before sprinting down the street. But I told myself I was only running, not because I was guilty, but because there was no way out of this. Jail time was not good for my complexion. Even if it wouldn't necessarily hurt my reputation. I just didn't need more water on a problem that was already growing.

Three blocks down, I stuck to the shadows and saw a man pulling into his driveway. The cops were just on my heel. I ran to the car and pulled open the door to the backseat, diving inside like it was a pool and closing the door behind me. "Don't move."

(End of Sneak Peek)

To continue reading the rest of the chapter, be sure to pick up the next

Honey Strait Novel:

THE PARRY GARDEN

About Author

Paige Lynn Hill is an entrepreneur and multifaceted author. As a businesswoman, Paige has spent half her life writing and now she gets to put a little romance into every pen stroke. She first became a lifelong writer and first began creating lovebirds in the seventh grade and published her first poem in high school. Her love of reading started even before then. However, life's interjections sent her into poetry and eventually business. But she managed to find her way back to her first love, writing novels. Propelled like everyone else by a terribly written TV show that used to be one of her favorites. She thought she could do better and then she did. Now it's all she loves to do.

Author Links:

Website: www.trsbooks.com

Facebook: www.facebook.com/authorpaigelynnhill

Instagram: https://www.instagram.com/authorpaigelynnhill

Newsletter: https://trsbooks.com/newsletter/